FREDERICK GRICE

The Oak and the Ash

ILLUSTRATED BY

TREVOR RIDLEY

with an afterword by Gaven Grice

OXFORD UNIVERSITY PRESS

Oxford   Toronto   Melbourne

Oxford University Press, Walton Street, Oxford OX2 6DP

Oxford New York Toronto
Delhi Bombay Calcutta Madras Karachi
Petaling Jaya Singapore Hong Kong Tokyo
Nairobi Dar es Salaam Cape Town
Melbourne Auckland

and associated companies in
Beirut Berlin Ibadan Nicosia

Oxford is a trade mark of Oxford University Press

First published 1986
First published in this edition 1986

© Frederick Grice 1968
Author's Afterword © Gwen Grice 1985

ISBN 0 19 271538 0

Printed and bound in Great Britain by
William Clowes Limited, Beccles and London

For

VERONICA

The oak and the ash, and the bonny ivy tree,
They flourish at home, in my ain countree.

(NORTH COUNTRY FOLK-SONG)

Acknowledgements

We are grateful to the following copyright holders for allowing us to use extracts from copyright material in this book:

(p. 20) 'At the Cross'. Reproduced by permission of The Salvation Army.

(p. 46) 'Thora', words by Fred E. Weatherley. Reproduced by permission of Boosey & Hawkes.

(p. 48) 'The Sunshine of Your Smile', words by Leonard Cooke. Reproduced by permission of Francis Day & Hunter Ltd.

Contents

Francis Makes a Blunder

THE classroom was very quiet. The twelve o'clock buzzer had gone, and all who were not taking the examination had gone to dinner. So had many of the candidates. Either because they had done as much as they could do, or like their fathers and mothers did not like the sense of being separated from their friends and fellows, most of the young examinees had handed in their papers and gone. Once outside the school they ran off into the streets like fish returned to the stream. Only a handful of boys was now left, and the only sounds in the room were the gurgling of the pipes, the scraping of hobnail boots on the iron crosspieces of the desks, and the scratching of pens. As the minutes ticked by, one more candidate gave in, and his rough

boots clattered over the floor of the classroom as he went up to
hand in his paper. In the end there was only one boy left. When
he looked up and found he was alone he felt a momentary pang
of alarm. He was too engrossed to be seriously troubled, but he
must have looked a little anxious because the teacher stirred and
spoke. It was Mr. Cresswell, a teacher whom the boys generally
feared. He was irritable and impatient and at times violent. Yet
when he spoke it was in a kind voice. ' Don't hurry, Kirtley.
The examination goes on until half-past. You have plenty of time
left.'

It was a pleasant surprise to hear him speak in so gentle a voice,
and the boy was suddenly inspired with a tremendous resolution,
almost with obstinacy. He would not be rushed. He hadn't
finished yet, but there was nothing wrong in not having finished.
The time was still his and he was determined to use it.

He worked quickly, looking up from time to time. In these
little intervals he did not seem to observe anything, yet everything imprinted itself upon his brain—the old stained map on the
wall, so dark and brown that hardly any detail could be seen on
it, the queer grain, like contour lines, on the cheap yellow cupboards, the long cobwebs hanging from the high ceiling, and
Mr. Cresswell's bent right arm, the arm that had been damaged
in the war. He looked down and returned to the last questions.

> ' Write down in your own words the meaning of
> the following proverbs :—
> " A rolling stone gathers no moss. . . ." '

It was difficult to find new words for that, but he wrestled
with his vocabulary and found an equivalent. He struggled with
all the proverbs and as the hand on the discoloured school clock
moved towards the half-hour, he ruled off and gave in his paper.
There was a moment of solitude as he stood, the only boy in the
great empty playground, but he pulled on his cap, kicked a stone
before him, and ran home.

As he drew near to home he could hear the familiar sounds of a colliery washing-day—the thumping of the poss-sticks in the wash-tubs, a rhythmic boom-boom as the wooden possers beat against the bottom of the tubs; and when he turned the corner he saw the lines of washing all strung out across the muddy streets. One of those poss-sticks being pounded up and down in the tub and one of those lines belonged to his mother.

When he got home he found her in a kitchen full of steam and the unpleasant odour of washing. The floor was covered with piles of dirty clothes, all sorted into whites and coloureds; and every flat space was occupied by her paraphernalia—scrubbing-brushes, tins of blue, bowls of starch, slabs of yellow soap, and pegs. Francis's mother was always in a disagreeable mood on washing-day; she was even more cross at his coming home at this inconvenient time.

'A nice day to pick for an examination, I must say,' she said. 'You would have thought they'd have enough sense to keep off a washing-day, at any rate. Well, you'll have to slip down to Mrs. Cairns', and get yourself a pie and a few peas, because I canna be bothered with you.'

He went for his pie and ate his dinner on a small space cleared on the kitchen table. He liked Mrs. Cairns's pies, but he did not like the smell of washing-day, and as soon as he could he went back to school.

He could not help wondering as he went back why Mr. Cresswell had been so kind to him. Mr. Cresswell was not his class-teacher, but sometimes he took them for Scripture. The last time he had taken them he had been in a furious temper. He had asked them all what this verse meant:

'The stone which the builders rejected is now become the head of the corner.'

Francis had tried hard to work out the meaning, but he had never seen anyone working in stone. Sometimes he had watched the colliery masons building a wall, or the men making a 'cree' for the pigeons, but he could not remember having seen anyone building with stone. In any case, what was the meaning of 'the head of the corner'?

How could a corner have a head? No one had known what the verse meant and Mr. Cresswell had been furious. Francis was vexed that he did not know, because sometimes sudden flashes of knowledge would come to him; but on this occasion he had been with the duffers. Mr. Cresswell had got more and more vexed, and he had hit Chris Ord with that curved right arm of his. Yet this morning he had been very gentle. Just when Francis had been growing alarmed at being left in the big examination room he had spoken a kind word.

The day after the examination the class was working quietly when the door in the partition opened and the Headmaster came in. He was wearing his spectacles and had some papers in his hand. He did not apologize to the teacher for interrupting the lesson, but pulled off his glasses and said abruptly, 'There's a boy here that's done something very stupid in his examination paper. Now who was the boy who answered all the questions on that English paper yesterday? Who was it?'

Francis had no doubt who the offender was. He suddenly realized why he had taken so long to finish, and all the pride that he had felt at making a good job of the examination went out of him. It hadn't been a great achievement after all. It had been just a great mistake. All that he had prided himself on was now being shown up as a silly blunder. His hand trembled as he lifted it. 'So that's the culprit, is it?' said the Headmaster. He must have known who it was, and have wanted to show him up before the rest of the class. As he stood in front of the class with his spectacles in one hand and the papers in the other, the Headmaster looked enormous and threatening.

'So it was you, was it? What's your name?'

'Francis Kirtley, sir.'

'Well, Francis Kirtley, get this into your head—if you won't read the instructions on your examination papers, you'll fail. It's happened before. I've seen it. I've seen a boy do that sort of trick and the examiners failed him. You've been very stupid, Francis Kirtley, haven't you?'

'Yes, sir.'

'Well, I can't hold out any hope for you. They don't want boys in the Secondary School that can't read instructions. I've seen it happen before and I won't be surprised if they turn you down.'

It was a strange thing but he did not seem particularly angry, or even in great earnest; but Francis was overwhelmed with shame, and when he sat down he was shaking. The boys were all giving him sidelong glances to see if he was going to blush or cry, but when the Headmaster had gone the teacher told them to get on quietly with their compositions, and Francis was left alone with his shame and his guilt. It was not that he was desperately anxious to go to the Secondary School. He had no idea what it was like there and didn't know anybody who went to it. But he hated doing anything badly, and he kept his head close to his book so that no one would see his humiliation.

2

The Side and the Broom

HESLEYSIDE was a colliery village of twenty or thirty rows of houses that sprawled over a windy hill-side a few miles to the north-west of the city of Durham. Below it ran the River Deerness, more like a beck than a river, narrow and fast-flowing, but polluted and grey like the water that Francis's mother emptied out of the tub when she had finished the washing. Alongside the river was a single-track railway. The railway stopped a few miles farther up the valley at Blackhouses, but the road went on over the fells towards the dales.

The fells were windy and lonely, scarred here and there with drifts and worked-out quarries. Along the ridge above the colliery straggled the village that had given the colliery its name, two rows of old houses, some of which had fallen down as the worked-out seams below them had caved in. No miners lived there. The few houses that had not collapsed were occupied by the men who worked on the fell farms. They had little to do with the pitmen, and the village seemed to stand apart as if it belonged to a different age.

Below the colliery, stretching on either side of the Deerness, was the Broom. It was little more than a mile away, but it, too, was a different world. It had no pit of its own, but the Hesley-side colliery manager lived there. So did some of the teachers, the insurance men, the people who worked in the Co-op, the railwaymen, and the shopkeepers. In Hesleyside there was not a single shop, and the women had to go to the Broom for every-thing they wanted.

There was little love lost between the people of the colliery and the people of the Broom, and the symbol of the barrier between them was the big slag heap that divided them. In the years since the first shaft had been sunk it had grown until it towered over the Broom like a black rampart. Some time ago, no one knew when, it had begun to smoulder. By day yellow fumes played on the surface, and on windy nights it would break out in flames. Everyone called it the Bleezer and the boys looked upon it as their playground. Behind it the people of Hesleyside lived their independent lives, with little time for either the slow-moving villagers above them or the better-off shop-keeping folk of the Broom below them.

The grown-ups of the Side and the Broom lived peaceably enough together, but the boys of the two communities lived in a state of constant feud, and fought as fiercely as if they belonged to two opposed and warring tribes.

Only a short time before the examination Francis had got the worst of a fight with some boys from the Broom. He had been sent there to do some shopping for his mother. He disliked shopping but he had an even greater dislike for a straw hat which his mother had made him wear. He felt silly in it, but he had to wear it because it was he who in a foolish moment had got his mother to buy it for him. As he went over the Bleezer he had a feeling that his 'straw benger' was going to bring him bad luck.

He managed to do the shopping without attracting too much notice, but as he was coming home with his basket he met three boys playing under the bridge that marked the frontier between the Side and the Broom. He knew that he was in for trouble when he noticed that one of them was a boy called Cutty Bilton. He had got the name because once in a stone-fight he had been hit on the right eyebrow. He had never managed to get rid of the scar. It was like a little white cut, as if somebody had taken a pair of scissors and snipped the eyebrow in two. He was a great bully and an enemy to all the boys from the colliery.

Francis tried to edge past the boys, but they made a line in front of him, jostling him and making fun of his straw hat.

' Straw benger, straw benger! ' shouted Bilton. ' Where did you get that fancy hat, eh ? '

Then he swept it off Francis's head and sent it spinning. Francis put down his basket and went for him, but one of the other boys tapped his ankles as he went forward and he tripped and fell. Then Bilton jumped on top of him, straddling him and pinning his arms above his head to the ground.

' Say this after me,' he said. ' Go on, say it—" I cry you mercy." '

' I won't,' said Francis.

" I cry you mercy, I grant you grace."

Francis wriggled and would not repeat the words, but Cutty went on :

> " I hope a little dog
> Will pittle in my face."

Then he bent down and spat and part of his spittle fell on Francis's brow. The other boys kicked over the basket of groceries and ran away laughing.

Francis picked himself up and collected his basket and his hat, wondering if the groceries had been damaged.

The feel of the spit on his brow made him feel angry. He hated spitting. He had often seen his uncle Jacob, his cousin's father, get out of his chair and spit in the fire, and the sound of the spittle sizzling on the coals disgusted him. He took out the rag that his mother had given him for a handkerchief, rubbed his brow and threw the rag away. He felt a little better when he had cleaned himself and got rid of the rag. Besides, although he had got the worst of the fight, he hadn't given in completely. He hadn't repeated the coward's formula, and the straw benger was so knocked about that he would never have to wear it again.

A few days later he got his revenge. He was out for a walk with his cousin David, looking for newts in the pond by the edge of the Bleezer. They didn't find any but they enjoyed themselves throwing stones into the water and floating logs across the pond. Then when they had finished they went off towards a little farm on the road towards Lowburn. Somebody had told them that there was a new farmer and he was deaf and dumb. If he saw you he made queer sounds to keep you off. They did not get as far as the farm, but on the road they came face to face with Cutty and another boy from the Broom.

' Hey, David,' said Francis. ' See who that is? It's Cutty. He's the one that got me down under the bridge and kicked the basket over.'

' Is it! ' said David. ' I've been waiting to have a go at him.'

' He's a good fighter.'

' I'm not frightened of him. It's time somebody settled his hash.'

He stepped into the middle of the road and waited till the
Broomies came up to him. They tried to edge past him.

'I've been waiting for you, Cutty Bilton. You knocked my
cousin down, didn't you?'

'I never meant nothing,' said Bilton, still trying to edge past.
'It was just a bit of fun.'

'Well, so's this,' said David. He pulled his jacket off and
threw it down on the grass verge.

'I didn't hurt him,' said Bilton. 'I never did nothing to him.'
But David did not listen to him.

'There's thy bat,' he said, going up to Bilton and pushing him
quite gently on the shoulder. 'There's thy chance,' he went on,

giving a second equally gentle push. ' And there's thy roasted teacake ! ' This time he hit him a bit harder. They all knew now that a challenge had been given, and Bilton would have to fight or be shown up as a coward. This was the formula all the boys used for a serious challenge.

Bilton put up his fists and came at David, but David was ready for him. He drew back and punched him hard on the breastbone and knocked him down.

Cutty picked himself up, but this time when he came in he had a stone in his hand. David caught him by the wrist and twisted it till he dropped the stone. Then he clouted him hard across the ear. Knowing now that he had met more than his match, Bilton lifted his leg to kick his opponent, but David knocked the leg up as it swung and he went down again. He got up once more and came in with his head down but another clout sent him to the ground again. He knew now that there was no escape except by flight, and began to look for a way to get past.

All the time David and Cutty were fighting, the other Broomie stood looking on. He made no move to join in, and although he was a biggish boy, Francis knew that he could beat him. He got behind him, collared him and pulled him down. Then he sat on him just as he had been straddled in the fight under the bridge.

' What should I do with him, David ? ' he said. He wanted to make him give in but he couldn't bring himself to do what the Broomies had done to him.

' Let him get up, Francis. . . . Go on, skedaddle, the pair of you. Get back to the Broom where you belong ! '

The two boys fled. When they were at a safe distance, they began to throw stones, but they were too far away to do any damage, and when David made a rush at them they disappeared round a bend in the road.

From then on neither Cutty nor his friends dared to set on Francis even when he was alone. He was a little ashamed that he had waited so long before joining in the scrap. Still it was a victory, even though it had been more David's doing than his.

3

Soldier From the War Returning

MR. AND MRS. KIRTLEY lived at 15 Russell Street. Although No. 15 was in the middle of the row it was a quiet house, with quiet neighbours; but from time to time the silence of the house was broken by strange noises. One was a mysterious scampering overhead. Mr. Kirtley said it was the mice that lived in the big loft that ran from one end of the street to the other. At times a sudden pattering could be heard, as if hundreds of them had made up their minds to move their quarters; then after a while they could be heard rushing back as if they had changed their minds after all.

The other noise was more solemn and alarming. It was a deep booming noise that seemed to come up from the centre of the earth. It was an ominous sound, faint but menacing. If you lay down on the kitchen floor with your ear to the ground you could hear it very plainly, like the sound of guns coming up from some underground battlefield. When Mr. Kirtley had told Francis that it was the sound of shots being fired in the seams far below the colliery, he was frightened, fearing that the explosions would some day come nearer and crack open the floor beneath him; but as he grew older and nothing disastrous happened, he grew used to the noise, and liked to lie on the cold floor, straining to hear more distinctly.

There were two large rooms downstairs, but ' the room ', as the sitting-room was called, was rarely used. The family spent most of their time in the kitchen, which was big and cosy. One of its sides was almost wholly taken up by a big kitchen range, with a wide cavernous fire-place that was constantly fed, summer and winter. Francis's father or mother would bring a big scuttle of coal from the coal-house in the yard, lift it, stand poised for a moment, then hurl the contents to the back of the big hollow fire. They were both expert at this, and the coal shot in a black cataract from the scuttle into the cavernous hollow behind the grate.

This fire was a thing with a life of its own. Sometimes, when the coal was bad, sharp explosions came from it as if it were angry, and little pieces of stone and metal would fly into the room. Then the big blazer would be put up until the explosions were over. When it had been burning for a long time, flakes of soot could be seen clinging loosely to the bars and flapping in the draught. Mrs. Kirtley called them 'strangers', and said they were a token that unexpected visitors were coming to the house. She would not rake them off, but looked upon them as good omens.

Sometimes when they came in late and the fire was low, she would spread a sheet of newspaper over the blazer to make a better draught; and if she forgot to watch it, it sometimes caught fire and there was a rush to stop the flames from spreading to the things that were hanging drying on the line under the mantelpiece.

But for most of the time the fire burned peacefully and comfortingly, with blue and orange flames reaching upward through the cracks in the crusted surface of the coal, and fiery caverns appeared in it, widening and opening into new vistas until, with a noise like a sigh, the fire fell inwards upon itself, and sparks flew upwards, disappearing into the blackness of the chimney.

Francis loved the fire. He loved to sit in front of it when he had finished reading, and pore upon the glowing caves that opened in its depths. It fed his imagination, and he seemed to see those crimson caverns peopled by strange creatures; and on cold mornings his mother would let him take his breakfast on the warm folded-down shelf of the oven, and put his feet inside the fender so that all his body drew in the comforting warmth of the fire.

Francis had neither brother nor sister, but there was a fourth member of the household, his mother's brother Thomas. Thomas

had come to live with them
not long after he had come
home from the prisoner-of-
war camp. He had been a
hewer, like Mr. Kirtley, but he
had been so badly wounded
that he could not go back to
the coal face. He was given a
light job in the Lamp Cabin,
and went into lodgings, but
Mr. Kirtley did not like the
idea of his having to live with
strangers. ' Ask your Tommy
if he would like to come and
live with us, Dot,' he said. ' I
dinna see why he should be
beholden to strangers when he
has relations in the place. Anyhow, it's not good enough.
Damn me, it's the least we can
do for the poor lad after all
he's had to gan through.'

Mrs. Kirtley was more than ready to take her brother in. She
put a bed for him in the attic, and he moved in.

Before Thomas came the attic had already contained its stock
of war souvenirs. All Mrs. Kirtley's brothers had sent her cards
from France, beautiful postcards unlike anything you could get
in England, made out of muslin and silk and embroidered with
coloured designs. There was one design that Francis was very
fond of—two arms in pink with fingers outlined in blue, reaching
out of nowhere and clasping firmly. Over the clasping hands
was embroidered ' Hands Across the Sea '.

Mrs. Kirtley had kept these cards and had even had some of
them framed, but they had never been put up. Now that the
war was over she had even less desire to put them up, and they
were left standing against the attic wall. There were also three

or four old copper shell cases, a clip of bullets and an old tin hat.

When Thomas arrived the collection was added to. He had kept his puttees, though he had no use for them, and he still had his greatcoat, which he liked to throw over the bed in cold weather. There were other treasures that he kept downstairs, among them two albums of photographs, mainly of comrades he had known in the prison camp; but some were of German guards and orderlies and doctors.

But he himself was the most vivid reminder of the war. He had been wounded in the upper part of the left leg, and was lame. His leg seemed to flap as he walked, and gave the impression that he imagined he was still on the parade ground and was trying to march. One day when he was getting bathed in front of the fire he showed Francis the scar. It was like a big blue bruise, and across the bruise you could see the long snaking line of the operation, crossed with big stitch marks.

Sometimes he would talk about the day when he had been wounded and had lain for two days in a shell hole until the Germans had picked him up, but he spoke less about his wound and his capture than about the friends he had made in the P.O.W. camp and the food he had had to eat. In a baccy tin he kept a little chunk of black bread, more like stone than bread, and he often took it out to show Francis.

There were some things of which he never spoke—his wife, his home and the few short weeks of married life he had enjoyed before he went to France; but Francis often heard his mother talking about it, and picking up a hint here and a detail there, he pieced the story together in his mind. Thomas had come home on his first leave to find an empty house. His wife had gone off, and nobody knew where. Every stick of furniture had been sold —every picture on the wall and every cup in the pantry. No one ever found out where his wife had gone. Since that time Thomas had never seen her. He had never even tried to find out where she was, and from then onwards he never thought of any other woman, except his sister, who had given him a home. He was not a miserable or moody man. He often used to make Francis laugh with his queer German phrases—'*Alleman kaputt*', '*Das Vaterland kaputt!*' etc.; but sometimes he would sit sad and silent, and it seemed to Francis then that he was thinking about his wife and the cold, empty house to which he returned from the trenches.

Mr. Kirtley had not served in the war. He was a strong man and never ailed, but the tribunals said he had a missing cartilage and they turned him down. He had worked in the pit all through the war, though all his wife's brothers had been soldiers and two of them had been killed. Their names were on the War Memorial outside the United Methodist Chapel.

Francis could not remember much about his dead uncles. He could vaguely remember being taken to Durham to meet them when they came on leave, and seeing his grandfather, who would never, even to welcome his sons home, enter a public house, waiting outside till they'd finished drinking. Francis had been taken inside, and remembered the floor littered with kitbags and bottles and rifles, and his uncles handing around tins of Woodbines. Then some time later he saw his mother crying over a letter, and after that his uncles never came on leave again.

But now it was nearly two years since the Armistice, and already he was beginning to forget how he had helped his mother to make home-made butter, and had been sent to the Broom to buy stone jars of rhubarb jam, and how he had been wakened one night to see a Zeppelin that had come raiding over Hartlepool. Nobody spoke much about the war now, but Francis liked to read about it, and spent hours poring over an illustrated history that his father had bought for him.

One day his uncle took him to Durham, and when they were in the park they saw two German tanks that had been taken in some action and presented to the city. They were open and you could go inside and look round them. Francis wished they had one in Hesleyside to play with, but his uncle was not interested in them. They reminded him too clearly of what he wanted to forget.

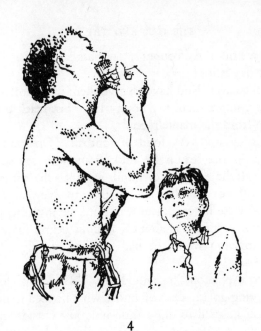

4

A Great Footballer

FRANCIS was sitting at the table with his legs astride the 'form'. This was his mother's name for the bench they used instead of kitchen chairs. He was watching his father shave. Mr. Kirtley was not tall, but he had very big shoulders. It was these shoulders that made him a good hewer. He was going bald, and brushed what hair he had left in a big sweep across his brow to hide his baldness; but he had a big moustache that swept outwards and upwards from the middle of his upper lip. After he had drunk anything he would sweep his moustache upwards first on one side and then on the other in a strange swaggering gesture.

Francis liked to watch his father shaving. As he scraped away with his safety razor his face took on strange comical expressions, but after his shave his skin always emerged with a surprising whiteness, drained of colour, like something kept from the sunshine, except for a few blue marks where the coal from explosions had embedded itself in his flesh.

' Shall we fill in the coupons, da ? ' asked Francis.

' What day is it ? '

' It's Thursday. You have to give them in tomorrow.'

' Right you are then, my bonny lad. Just reach the pen and ink down from the mantelpiece.'

Mr. Kirtley was very fond of football. On most Saturday afternoons in the season he took Francis to see some game or other. If he had had a good week at the pit they went to Newcastle or Sunderland—mainly to Newcastle, for the ' Magpies ' were his favourite team, and he loved to tell stories about them, particularly about a famous centre-forward called Sammy Appleton whom he had watched playing in the years before the war.

' Sammy Appleton,' he would say. ' Gee-whiz, he was the lad for scoring goals. Do you know what he used to do ? Afore the kick-off he used to dig a little hole just outside the penalty area and put an aspirin in it. And he nivver shifted mair than a few yards away from that aspirin.'

' What if he was off side ? '

' Off side ? You nivver caught that lad off side. He nivver used to run for the ball—blow me, I dinna think the feller could run. He just used to rely on his mates to give him the ball. And once he got it, he used to let fly. Like a gun, man, straight between the posts. Lad, I've nivver seen anybody score goals like him.'

The story of the aspirin always puzzled Francis. He could never quite understand what that little white pill had to do with scoring goals ; but it made the famous Sammy Appleton less like the players he had seen than a figure in a legend, a wizard who had turned goal-scoring into magic.

They began to look through the list of the teams. There were some of the names that had a wonderful ring to Francis's ears— Plymouth Argyle, Spurs, Heart of Midlothian, Queen of the South, Tranmere and Hamilton Academicals. He never thought of them as real places, as Durham and Chester-le-Street were real, places where there were mines and schools and shops, but as mysterious localities giving their names to clubs of fabulous fame. They were musical names that seemed to string themselves together for him like the words of a poem. He liked nothing better than to look for their places in the table, to read about their performances, to hear his father talk about their fortunes, and to mark down those whose week-end games would bring more fame to them and lucky wins for his father.

' Do you think our David will ever play for one of these teams, da ? ' he asked when they had finished marking the coupon.

' As sure as I'm standing here. Do you know that he's in the running for his cap ? '

' His county cap ? '

' That's what the men are saying. The scouts have been to see him already. He'll be in the county side afore the season is finished. And by gum he's worth his place. He's the best schoolboy footballer I've ever seen.'

A county cap ! No one from Hesleyside had ever won an honour like this. Francis was filled with pride at the thought that of all people his own cousin should earn such a distinction.

' But dinna mention it to him, Francis, will tha ? ' went on his father. ' I dinna want the lad to be disappointed if it falls through.'

' I won't, da,' said Francis, but he wondered how he could possibly keep so valuable a secret to himself.

The next night he went to see his cousin, to find out if there was any more news. He knew that he would keep the word he had given to his father. He had a strong sense of honour and did not easily betray a confidence, but he was restless for more news.

His aunt Elizabeth was standing ironing when he went in. At first he thought that she was alone, but a noise from the back room told him that her husband was there. He could hear him banging away at the piano, thumping the keys with his heavy fingers. He was playing a hymn. He went through the melody and suddenly burst out in a loud, jarring voice—

> ' We have an anchor that keeps the soul
> Steadfast and sure while the billows roll,
> Fasten'd to the Rock which cannot move,
> Grounded firm and deep in the Saviour's love.'

He sang noisily, as if he were trying to make the walls, the furniture, the piano itself join in with him. Francis saw his aunt look up from her ironing and sigh. Her husband's presence always irritated her, and she did not like to have the quiet of the house disturbed by his noisy singing.

' He has a voice like a foghorn,' she said, frowning. ' But come in, Francis, and tell us the news—if you can make yourself heard.'

' I've just come to see David, Aunt Elizabeth.'

' I'm afraid he's still at the band practice, Francis. But he should be back any minute . . . Heavens above, listen to that noise. You'd think he was trying to bring the house down, wouldn't you?'

Her husband had turned to an even noisier hymn:

> ' At the Cross, at the Cross, where I first saw the light,
> And the burden of my heart rolled away,
> It was there, by faith, I received my sight,
> And now I am happy all the day.'

He seemed to enjoy the tune. He sang it again and then broke into—

> ' Who is He that's knocking, knocking?
> Knocking at the door . . .'

Francis did not mind his uncle's singing. His mother and father never sang hymns, but he had often heard people at Chapel singing with the same kind of voice. He thought it was the proper way to sing hymns.

He sat down to wait for David and watched his aunt. She was ironing on a big white sheet that she had laid over the kitchen table. Raking among the hot coals she hooked out a red-hot bar with her poker and dropped it neatly into her iron. Then, wetting her finger and dabbing it quickly on the bottom of the iron to test the heat, she began to pass it quickly backwards and forwards over the blouse she was ironing. He saw it folding into neat little frills.

From behind the wall hymn followed hymn, with no slackening of volume.

' What sort of ironing is that, Aunt Elizabeth ? '

' It's goffering.'

' Where did you learn to do that ? At school ? '

' No. I learnt it when I was in service. I wasn't always a pitman's wife, you know,' she went on with a touch of pride. ' I was a laundrymaid once in a big house—in a castle.'

' A real castle ? '

' Yes, but that was a long time since. I've nearly forgotten what it was like. Would you like to do a job for David while you're waiting ? '

' Yes, I would.'

' Well I know he wants his football boots dubbined in time for the game on Friday, and he would have done them himself if he hadn't had to go to the practice.'

' I'll do them, Aunt Elizabeth.'

' Will you ? He'll be bonny and pleased if he comes back and sees them finished.'

It was a greasy job, but he would have done anything to please David. He took out the laces, washed them and hung them out to dry, and then began working the dubbin into the hard leather. While he was busy, he heard his uncle bang down the piano lid, yawn noisily, ending his yawn as he always did with an ' Aye, aye, aye, aye ', and come into the kitchen. He was in his shirt sleeves, with his waistcoat unbuttoned, and his habitual foolish look on his face.

' Is that our Frankie ? ' he said. He spoke as loudly as he sang, as if he were hailing his nephew from the far side of the street.

' How's thi father gettin' on this week ? What sort of a place hes he got this quarter ? And what's that tha's busy with ? '

He put his questions one after the other without waiting for an answer. Francis did not know quite what to reply, but answered the last question. 'I'm getting David's boots ready for the game on Friday.'

'Pah, football, football! I think ye're all daft on football these days.'

'The lads have to have their sport, Jacob,' said his wife patiently.

'And your father's as bad as the rest,' he went on. He rarely listened to anything but the sound of his own voice. 'Encouraging young lads to think there's nowt in the world but a game of football.'

'I'm sure that he does no such thing.'

'By sangs, I've seen plenty of young fellers breaking their necks to get into a football jersey—aye, and a few months later they're fallin' ower theirsels to get back into the pit. So dinna think ye can make a fortune just out of kicking a ball about.'

'Francis has no such idea, and neither has David.'

Her husband took no notice of her reply.

'Aye, aye, aye, aye,' he said, finishing off another yawn. 'I think I'll just away down to the Institute for a few minutes.'

'What about your supper?'

'Oh just leave me a bit of bread and dripping. That's all I need,' and he pulled on his jacket and went out. His wife winced as he banged the door shut after him.

Francis went on greasing his cousin's boots, 'raxing' them to make them supple, and his aunt went backwards and forwards between table and fire, changing irons, folding the newly ironed clothes and stacking them on the table. Then they heard the yard gate open, and the kitchen sneck click, and David came in, his fair skin glowing with the evening walk, and his fair hair damped and stained with the drizzle.

The mood of the house seemed to change as soon as he came into it; but that was what seemed to happen wherever he went. He was his mother's son, as affectionate as his father was rough and noisy; and he had inherited his mother's good looks and good manners. In his company everyone seemed to unbend, to put aside their quarrels and anger, and to show the better side of their nature. Francis forgot that only a few days ago he had made a mess of his examination paper, and his aunt that she was married to a noisy, fatuous husband who would come back looking for the bread and dripping that he liked for his supper.

David said nothing about the cap, but Francis was not disappointed. He knew that sooner or later his cousin would be in the county team.

5

The Rebel

WIDE, unpaved, dusty in dry weather and muddy after rain, the street was the boys' main playground. It was their meeting-place, football pitch and battleground, with its own pleasures and dangers. There was a bearded old overman who lived behind a big brick wall in the end house, a bad-tempered man who hated boys and set his dogs on them if they tried to get into his garden to retrieve a lost ball. There were angry, houseproud wives who rushed out as soon as a ball was kicked into their yard, and refused to give it up. There were the constant hazards of coalmen, midden carts, and hawkers, and the policeman, a dread apparition before whom the boys all scattered. Every boy, fresh from some misdeed or other, fled at his approach as if merely to be seen by him was to be accused.

But there was one man who struck even greater terror into them than the policeman. He was a great shambling giant of a fellow who went by the name of Manny Pecker. Hardly anyone had seen him at close quarters. The cry that he was coming was enough to make them take to their heels before anyone could come face to face with him. Francis had caught no more than a glance of his great lurching figure, with its rough woollen cap pulled like a balaclava over his knobbly head, his face as rough as a bush, his half-witted, shambling way of walking. The boys told stories of his strange ways, his habit of spending his days picking over the place where the middens were emptied, the dirty places where he slept, the horrible unnatural food that he ate, and his habit of kidnapping boys, like some monster who came over the moors in search of bones and flesh.

As soon as the cry was raised—'Here's Manny Pecker!'—

they did not stop to see what he was up to but scattered, to come together only after the danger had passed. He was the wild bogy-man of their dreams, the creature that no one dared to confront or speak to.

Exciting though it was by day, the street was even more mysterious by night. In the hours between the falling of darkness and the time when their mothers came to the doors to call their sons in to supper and bed, the boys played their long repertoire of games—Kick the Block, Bump the Cuddy, Barley Biscuits, Bowly in Cap, Cappie on Deck, Knocky Nine Door and Jack Shine the Muggie. The best of all these games was the last, although it was not often that they played it for it was not easy to lay hands on a lamp or a 'muggie'. But sometimes one of the gang would turn up with an old lamp with a socket for a piece of candle and a reflector.

Jack Shine the Muggie was a 'searching' game. The boys who were to hide set down the lantern in a ring scored on the ground by the heel of somebody's boot. Then they ran off to their hiding-places and began to call out in the dark, 'Jack Shine the Muggie!' This was the sign for the boy who was the searcher to run out, pick up the lamp, and begin to call out—

'Give an 'oller, give an 'oller!'

The boys who were in hiding had to reply, disguising their voices but echoing the sound—

''Oller! 'Oller! 'Oller!'

It was a dark and secret game that Francis loved playing. He loved to be the searcher, the man with the lamp, hunting out the hidden ones, flashing the lamp on their faces and clapping his hand on their shoulders to signify that they were caught. He hated the moment when the candle-end they had stuck in the socket dissolved in a little pool of grease and they had to think of another game.

Francis was never at a loss for something or for someone to keep him company, but he liked best of all to play with a boy called Nocky Howden whose father and mother had come to live in Russell Street just after the war. His proper name was Enoch, but no one ever used it except the teachers. He was a reckless and forward boy, always in mischief, nosing round the pithead, stealing sour green apples from the farms on the edge of the colliery, lighting fires in the street and keeping them going with stolen coal. Mrs. Kirtley did not like him and was constantly warning Francis against him, but he was always up to something new, climbing through windows, squeezing his way through gaps in garden railings, exploring tunnels and ' cundies '. Besides he possessed a magic lantern and used to give little shows in the lavatory, throwing the pictures on a board that he had nailed to the door. Francis liked sitting huddled there in the darkness sniffing the smell of the candle and watching the slides. When they were not looking at the slides they were roaming up and down the dark streets, banging gates and knocking on doors, or lighting paper in the rain-water pipes until the draught made a fearful roaring sound that made the women come running out to see what was burning.

Francis liked going with Nocky, but he didn't like stealing, and wouldn't go with him when he went trespassing in the colliery yard. Sometimes Nocky would go into one of the little sweetshops that women kept in their houses and ask if they had any Wild Woodbines. When the women said yes, he would shout, ' Why don't you tame them ? ', and run out; but Francis did not like that sort of trick and wouldn't go into the shop with him.

Francis went with Nocky because they were both born wanderers, and were always getting into trouble for being missing just when they were wanted. In the first summer after the war there was an influenza epidemic. The school was closed and the summer holiday went on into September. Nobody in the Kirtley family caught the 'flu, and Francis made the most of his freedom. One day Nocky enticed him away to see a handball match at Lowburn, a colliery five or six miles away. It was a special match and Sandy Mordue, who played football for New-castle, was taking part in it. Francis knew that his mother would not let him go if he asked her permission, so the two of them took French leave.

It was a great game. It was played against the wall of a little public house called the ' Nicky Nack '. The house-end had been enlarged to make a handball wall, and before it was a big court, not paved, but flat and hard. The spectators stood behind the wooden railing that enclosed the court. The great Mordue was in fine form. He took on player after player, and in one game he was driving the ball so far back into the court that the men began to pull up the railings to let his opponent get to the ball. The men were noisy, betting heavily and shouting to the barman who went endlessly backwards and forwards between the alley and the pub with trays of beer. It was so exciting that Francis forgot, as he so often did, how late it was and how far he was from home. By the time the game was over and Nocky and he had got back to Hesleyside it was dark.

' Where on earth have you been ? ' said his mother when he came in. ' Have you seen your da ? '

' No.'

' He's been looking everywhere for you. Where have you been ? '

' I've been to see the handball game at Lowburn.'

' What, at this time of night ? '

' We had to walk home.'

' Why didn't you come and tell us you were off to Lowburn ? You daft little beggar, you're forever doing this trick ! Wander-ing off and never tellin' anybody where you're off to. I don't know where you get it from—stravaiging around the country-side at all hours of the day and night. Well, you've done it once too often this time ! And you'd better get out of sight before your father comes. 'Cos when he comes in there'll be ructions.'

His father was very vexed with him. There had been a meeting in the Union hut. The men were drawing lots for their ' cavils ', their working places in the pit, and Mr. Kirtley had spent so long searching for Francis that he had been late for the draw.

But not even the good talking-to his father gave him the next day cured him of his habit of wandering. Time and time again, alone or in company, he went straying off, not into other collieries, for the boys there were hostile towards strangers, but into the fields and quarries beyond the village, along the banks of the Deerness, and sometimes on to the fells. His mother gave him up, contenting herself with the remark that one day he'd wander off and never come back, and when he did it was no good expecting her to come hunting for him.

6

Nocky Goes into Hiding

TIME and time again Francis found himself in trouble for wandering off without letting his mother know where he was going.

' You're supposed to have some brains,' she would say, ' but I think you leave them behind you when you get with that Nocky Howden. You cause me mair trouble than a dozen lasses. It's time you stopped going around with him.'

' What's the matter with him ? '

' He's up to no good. He's got a wicked look on his face. He's always up to some mischief or other. He'll get into trouble one of these days, and you'll be with him if you don't watch out.'

' He doesn't do anything wrong, Mother.'

' I'm not so sure about that. I've heard some queer things about him and his carryings-on. He'll have the bobby after him if he doesn't watch his p's and q's.'

Francis always stuck up for his friend, but at heart he knew that she was right. Nocky was too fond of trespassing on other people's property and helping himself to things that did not belong to him. So far he had not been found out, but one day the colliery policeman, Mr. Cotterell, was seen in school, and word went round that Nocky had been caught stealing planks from the timber stack in the colliery yard. He was called out of class to go to the Headmaster, and didn't come back. They said that he had been sent home, but he didn't turn up for his tea. He didn't turn up at home that night, and the next day Mrs. Howden came to Mrs. Kirtley's to ask if Francis knew where he was. By now Mr. Howden had heard about the summons, and was making no secret of what he would do to his boy when he laid hands on him.

Francis pretended not to know where Nocky was. In a way it was no pretence, for he had not seen him since he had been called out of the classroom, but he remembered that Nocky had once told him that if he got into trouble he meant to hide in the drift on the fells until it had all blown over. He was afraid of his father, and did not dare to face him until he had calmed down.

Francis made up his mind that he would try to find Nocky and tell him how worried his mother was about him. He did not dare to steal much food from the pantry but when he came home at midday he managed to cut a thick slice from the loaf without being found out, and before he went back to school he bought a pie from Mrs. Cairns with threepence that his aunt Elizabeth had given him for doing a job for her. He filled a lemonade bottle with water and hid both the food and the drink in the wash-house. After tea he picked up his things and went to the drift. He had a torch that his mother had bought for his birthday. The battery wasn't much good, but it was still giving a light.

It had been raining earlier in the day and the ground at the mouth of the drift was soft and spongy; inside the hollow the water had dripped and collected in rusty pools. Francis knew

that if he was not careful he would dirty his boots and his mother would ask him where he had been to get them in that state. He thought of taking them off and going barefoot but it was too cold. Instead he collected a few loose stones and bricks and threw them down so that he could use them as stepping-stones. Then, switching on his torch, he began to feel his way along the tunnel, testing the ground at every step and keeping to the dry edges of the wagon way. Presently he came to a little stretch of rails that had not been taken up and went forward, balancing himself on them.

It was dark and silent except for the occasional drip of water from the neglected roof, but looking back he could still see the drift, an irregular oval of light dwindling behind him, and before him the rays of his torch fell on the seams and strata of coal and rock. With every step the darkness and silence grew, and he felt an impulse to turn back from the suffocating blackness before him, but he felt certain that somewhere in the tunnel he would find Nocky.

He paused to swing his torch, and in the silence he thought he heard someone get cautiously to his feet and move away in front of him.

'Nocky!' he called. 'Are you there?'

Nothing answered him but the eerie echoing of his own voice. He went forward, not minding now where he put his feet, and when he paused a second time to throw the beam of his torch farther ahead, he heard once more the stealthy sound of someone scuffling away ahead of him.

'Nocky! Nocky!' he called out. 'Don't be frightened—it's just me—Francis.'

Again there was no reply. Francis switched off his torch and moved forward softly, keeping one hand on the wall of the drift. Then when he felt that he had turned a corner, he switched it on again, and saw Nocky. He was sitting huddled in a niche in the wall, a little hollowed-out shelter where the men used to withdraw to keep out of the way of the passing tubs.

'Nocky,' he said. 'They're looking everywhere for you.'

'I'm not coming,' said Nocky. 'I'll get wrong from my father. He'll hit me.'

'They want you to come back.'

' I'm not coming.'

' I brought you something to eat, Nocky. Some bread and a pie. Do you want them ? '

' Yes. I'm starved.'

' But you can't stop here.'

' I can. It isn't cold, you know. I wasn't cold last night.'

' You can't stay for always.'

' I'm going to stop here till my father says he'll leave me alone.'

' Come on now ! '

' No.'

' I'll have to go back, Nocky. The battery's nearly finished. What have I to say when they ask me ? '

' Don't tell anybody where I am. But I'll come out if my father says he'll leave me alone.'

' I'll have to go. Are you frightened here by yourself ? '

' I'm not frightened here, but I'm frightened of my father. Can you bring me another pie, Francis ? '

' I'll try.'

But by this time his torch was beginning to fail. The light was turning yellow and feeble. He hurried out of the drift, picking his way carefully across the stones he had laid down. His boots were dirtier than he had meant to get them but he pulled up handfuls of wet grass and rubbed them clean. When he got home he had time to blacken and polish them before his mother came in, and she did not ask him where he had been.

When a second night had passed and Nocky had still not come home, word went round the colliery that the police were going to start a search for him. They had sent his description to every police-station in the county, and were thinking of dragging the pond. Francis tried hard to keep his mind on his work, but he kept thinking of Nocky. He hardly knew what was said to him and what he was answering and almost got the cane for being stupid. Then as he was coming out of school at tea-time, he saw the caretaker taking the ropes and hooks from the boiler-house where he always kept them, and he knew that the men were going to start dragging the pond.

During tea Francis kept his eye on his father. He knew that he would have to speak to him but he kept putting it off until the last minute. At last, when his father had pushed back his chair and reached for his jacket, Francis said, 'Are you going to help with the dragging, da?'

'I'm going to be there to give a hand—although I'm not looking forward to it.'

'It won't be any good.'

'What won't be any good?'

'Dragging the pond.'

'And why not?'

'Because Nocky isn't there.'

'He hasn't done away with himself then?' asked Mrs. Kirtley.

'No.'

'Well, you'd better tell his mother—and double quick,' she said. 'Poor soul, she's been nearly beside herself with worry about him. Where is he? What's the matter with you? Don't you know where he is?'

'Yes, I know, Mother, but I cannot tell you.'

'And why not?'

'I told Nocky I wouldn't give him away until his father had promised not to give him a hiding.'

'Nay, Francis, this isn't good enough. There's both Mr. and Mrs. Howden at their wits' end, and all the policemen in the county looking out for this lad.'

'I still can't tell you, da.'

'I know you can be obstinate, Francis, but this is beyond a joke. Come on, be reasonable.'

'I'll tell Mr. Howden if he promises not to punish Nocky.'

'You stubborn little hoit!' said his mother. But Mr. Kirtley stopped her.

'The best thing is to fetch Matty here and bring him face to face with the bairn. I'll tell Sarah that her lad's safe enough—and that'll be as good as a golden sovereign for her.'

A few minutes later he came back with both Mr. and Mrs. Howden. Mrs. Kirtley made Mrs. Howden sit down in front of the fire, but Mr. Howden, with the awkwardness of a miner in an unfamiliar house, remained standing. He was a big man, with a rough, raw complexion, and blue rings tattooed round his big bony fingers.

'Tha's lifted a load off my mind, hinny,' said Mrs. Howden to Francis, ' but I winna rest till I know where he is.'

'I cannot tell you, Mrs. Howden, until Mr. Howden has promised.'

'Promised? By sangs, when I lay hands on that boy I'll pay him back for all the trouble he's caused me these last two days.'

'Nay, Matty, dinna talk like that,' pleaded his wife.

'I'll talk the way I like,' he went on. 'Come on, lad, where is he?'

But Francis would not speak. Looking at the ugly raw-faced man before him, he knew that he would rather be beaten himself than give in.

'That's not the way to talk to him, Matty,' said Mr. Kirtley. 'You'll get nothing out of him by bawling and yelling.'

'I'd get something out of him if he was mine.'

'Oh, for heaven's sake, Matty,' said his wife. 'Try to see the lad's point of view. You'll tell us, won't you, Francis?'

'Yes, when Mr. Howden has given his word.'

'Come on, let bygones be bygones, Matty,' said Mr. Kirtley. 'You'll do the lad a sight mair good by forgiving him than by taking the stick to him. Give thy word, man.'

'All right then, I'll give it,' said Mr. Howden, with an effort. 'Where is he?'

'He's in the big drift up past the village.'

Straker's drift?'

'Yes.'

'Hes he been there all the time?' asked Mrs. Howden.

'Yes.'

'Poor bairn, he'll be starved to death.'

'No, he's had something to eat and drink, Mrs. Howden. I took him a pie and some bread.'

'That was very nice of you, hinny, and I'll nivver forget it.'

'Let's get him out as soon as possible,' said Mr. Howden.

'Just pop something to eat in my bait poke, Dot,' said Mr. Kirtley, 'and fill him a drop of tea in my pit bottle. And put thy coat on, Francis, and come with us.'

Once more Francis went alone into the drift. He had not to go so far this time. He found Nocky crouching close to the entrance. Hunger, loneliness and darkness had begun to tell on him. Once he heard that his father did not mean to hurt him, he gave in. He was anxious to be home. When the two boys emerged no one spoke. No one could find anything fitting to say.

In silence they all walked down the hill, but when they came to the place where they had to part company, Francis pulled his father's sleeve and whispered, 'Remind Mr. Howden what he promised, da.' But his father replied, 'Nay, lad, I've interfered enough. It's time you were getting back to your mother. She'll not be easy in her mind till she knows we've got him back.'

Mrs. Kirtley sent Francis off to bed, but not before she had reminded him of what she had said many a time to him before.

'I hope you're satisfied now. I told you that lad would get you into trouble. I don't know what the police will say when they get to know about this. I don't know where you get this obstinacy from. I'm sure it's not from my side.' But his father stuck up for him.

'Let it drop, Dot,' he said, 'and just be thankful that ivverything's turned out the way it has. He might be obstinate but if it hadn't been for him Nocky would have been a sight worse than he is.'

7

The Fight with the Broomies

MR. HOWDEN did not keep his word. Nocky told Francis that his father had begun by giving him a good telling-off, then he had lost his temper and beaten him with his pit belt. After this Francis did not go often to call on Nocky, because he could hardly bear the sight of the ugly raw-faced man who had deceived him, but the boys were still friends and from to time went off together, even though Nocky had had a summons.

As the time went on Francis went more and more often to see his cousin. It was David's last year at school and Mr. Cresswell had made him captain of the football team. He was very serious about football, and was training at night by going out for a run up to the village and back. Francis used to help his aunt Elizabeth to get the bath ready for him when he got back.

While he was waiting for David he talked with his aunt. She was very pretty—Mrs. Kirtley used to say she was the Mary to her Martha—and everything about her was neat. She was very good to Francis, taking out all her souvenirs of the days when she had been in service and showing them to him. She had four or five special books with covers made of fine wood. Her old mistress who had given her them had told her that it was olive wood from the Garden of Gethsemane in Jerusalem. The print was very small but Francis could still read it. Best of all he liked a little sketch-book that the lady had given his aunt just before she left. It was bound in dull red leather, and had a special metal clasp ; and the pages were covered with pencil drawings of cattle feeding in the park, trees and walks, and the castle itself with its terraces and battlements. Sometimes his aunt would let him take the book home and try to copy the sketches, and after a while he grew skilful at drawing trees and cows.

But the worst of the winter had not yet set in, and most of his spare time was spent, as always, out of doors.

One day during the short October holiday he went off with Chris and Billy Ord to play on a piece of waste ground near the railway that divided Hesleyside from the Broom, and while they were trying to start a fire in one of the hollows they saw a gang of boys from the Broom mustering in the field at the foot of the Bleezer. The Bleezer was not their territory, but from time to time they raided it. It was a triumph for them to get to the top without being driven back; to hold the summit, even for a few minutes, was a victory.

Peeping over the edge of the crater in which they were hiding, Francis saw the boys crossing the field and beginning to scale the slope. In front, leading them, was Bilton, out for revenge for the hiding David had given him. Francis saw him scramble up the scree, get to the crest and wave the rest on to follow him.

For a few moments it looked as if the Broomies were going to have it all their own way. They began to lark about, shouting and climbing on the old wagons that were used to bring the slag from the pithead; but suddenly Francis saw them running for shelter, and he knew that the counter-attack had begun. He saw Nocky appear on the skyline, picking up stones and firing them as he ran, and after him came David and a gang of twenty or thirty, leaping over the craters and the ditches and firing volley after volley.

It was not easy to dislodge the Broomies. The surface of the Bleezer was pock-marked with the craters made by the men who came to seek loose coal there during strikes. The hollows were like shell holes, and it was simple to lie down in them and let the stones fly harmlessly overhead, or to take shelter behind the old wagons. It was difficult to seize the Bleezer, but not so hard to hold it once it had been taken.

But although the Broomies had not been repelled, they had been edged away to the far end of the heap where the slope was not so steep, and their retreat gave Francis a chance to intervene.

' Let's get round the back of them,' he said to Chris and Billy, and, bending low, he ran around the edge of the field until he had put the invaders between him and Nocky's men. They loaded their pockets and fists with ammunition, and then leapt forward and began to let fly.

This was the first turning point in the battle.

When the surprised Broomies turned to face this new attack, Nocky and David and a dozen others jumped up from their holes and charged. Francis could hear the stones rattling against the sides of the trucks, and he heard one boy shout when he was hit. The double attack was too much for Bilton and his gang. They fled, leaping down the scree-like slope of the Bleezer, slithering and sliding until they had reached the safety of the field below.

Then followed a pause in the action, in which neither side made a move, although they all stood in full view of one another. It was now time to bandy insults.

Nocky began the exchange:

> ' Broom bugs, cock up your lugs
> And let the Siders pass you!'

And the Broom boys replied:

> ' Side bugs, cock up *your* lugs
> And let the Broomies pass *you*!'

Then one of them, seeing Nocky, began to shout in a mocking sing-song, 'There's Nocky Bulltrucks, there's Nocky Bulltrucks, there's Nocky Bulltrucks!', and the others joined in with him.

They could not have chosen a worse insult. Nocky didn't mind his ordinary nickname, but he always grew mad when he was called Bulltrucks, although no one knew for certain how he had been given it and why it riled him so much.

' Charge!' he shouted, bending down and filling his left fist with stones. ' Come on, get them! Charge!'

He took one flying leap down the slope, his heels sinking into the loose scree and his long body almost overtoppling in the violence of his plunge, but even as he leapt he flung his first stone,

and after him came the full Hesleyside force, leaping and slithering and sending the scree down in small black avalanches as if
they were driving the heap itself to overwhelm the enemy.

It was a rash manoeuvre, for it meant abandoning not only
their own territory but also their advantage. If the Broomies
had been able to outflank them they might have regained the
heap and the day would have been theirs. But the violence of
Nocky's charge was too much for them. They turned and fled,
locking their arms behind their necks and tucking their heads in
to protect themselves from the shower of stones that followed
them. The farther they ran the farther they retreated from their
supply of ammunition. There were stones of all sizes and shapes
on the heap, but on the field a stone big enough to throw was as
rare as a mushroom. Completely routed, the Broomies ran off
yelling until they had all disappeared over the railway line that
was the frontier and had been driven back into their own
territory.

It was a great victory, and as they scrambled back up the slope
of the Bleezer the boys laughed and shouted, boasting of the
number of hits they had made, and making fun of the undignified
retreat of their enemies. They hung round Nocky, slapping his
back and touching his jacket; and David came over to Francis
and put his arm round his shoulder. 'Well done, kidder!' he
said. 'You put the wind up them, Francis. You made them
run, didn't you?'

It was only when the battle was over and the boys were on
their way back to the colliery that Francis noticed he was bleed-
ing. A stone must have hit him just below the knee. He tried to
get rid of the cut by spitting on his handkerchief and rubbing with
it; but his mother spied it.

'What's this? You been fighting with stones again? Well,
you'd better get some iodine on that or else it will fester.'

He flinched as she spilt the iodine over the wound. The cure
was far more painful than the hurt. But he was proud of having
a wound and went around wearing the big iodine stain as if it
were a medal.

8

The Grandfather

WHEN Francis's father began to complain about a pain in his back, his wife said, ' Well, you'd better see if Grandpa has any more of them pills he gave you last time. They do you more good than anything else. Francis! Just pop up to your grandad's and ask if he can give your da a few pills, will you?'

Francis's grandfather, his mother's father, lived by himself in the Aged Miners' Homes. His wife had died a long time ago, but he refused to come and live with either of his daughters. Now, although he was over ninety, he cooked and cleaned for himself, refusing to take a ride on the new buses that were coming into use, but walking everywhere, looking less like a miner than a wandering preacher walking from gathering to gathering.

Francis lifted the sneck and walked into his kitchen. The old man barely looked up as he went in, but turned back to his book.

Every night, no matter what else he had been doing, he read a chapter of the Bible. Chapter by chapter he worked his way through the book, and when he came to the end he gave thanks and began again. It was his family Bible, bound in a shiny black leathery cover that he polished as carefully as he polished his own shoes. The thick black covers had a rim of brass, and there was a big clasp of the same metal that held the hard covers together. The brass rims were a bit dented in places, but they were very shiny. The print was very black and clear and the illustrations were in bright, glaring colours.

Francis sat down opposite his grandfather and watched him go on with his reading. The old man went very slowly, moving his lips almost inaudibly and following each word with his finger. Every now and then he sighed, either because the effort of read-

ing so closely and deliberately was tiring him or because something in what he read moved him.

He was very old. The light fell on his clean, bony face, revealing the little patches of dry skin on his cheeks, like little sores that would not heal. The space between the joints of his fingers was thin and white, as if the flesh had melted away from it.

He finished the chapter, folded the silk bookmark down and murmured something to himself. ' There now, Francis,' he said. ' There's one more chapter finished, and thanks be to the Saviour that has spared me to read one more wonderful story from the Scriptures. Now, my bonny lad, what's brought you up here tonight ? '

Francis was so busy looking at the book, wondering how far his grandfather had got, that he hardly heard what was said to him. Instead he asked, ' Have you read the Bible right through, Grandpa ? '

' Yes, from the first to the last.'

' More than once ? '

' Many times, many times. And I never tire of it.'

It seemed to Francis to be an extraordinary feat to read the Bible even once from end to end. Looking at the closed book on the table before him, he could not believe how anyone could have the patience to read this enormous volume from cover to cover, let alone an old man who read as slowly as his grandfather did, pointing with his finger to every word.

' But what's brought you up here tonight ? ' repeated the old man. ' Is there anything wrong at home ? '

' It's my da. He's got a bad back again, and he wants to know if you can give him a few pills.'

' Pills, eh ? Aye, he can have a few pills if that's what he wants. But I can tell him what will do him more good than pills.'

' What's that ? '

' Give up that bad habit of his of pouring strong liquor into himself. Give up his blessed Aitchies and his Guinnesses and his Youngers—the very names are an abomination to me—that's what's wrong with him.'

' He didn't get his bad back at the Club, Grandda. He got it at work.'

' Aye, that's what they all say. But I've worked in the pit and I've worked as hard as the best, but I never got a bad back. Because I didn't poison my system, the way they poison theirs. . . . Still, I'll give him the pills—and I'll give him a piece of my mind as well, when I see him.'

He lifted his Bible from the table, and put it in the place where he always kept it in between his readings, on the top of a chest of drawers by the wall. Then he took the soft cover from the table, laid down a roll of oilcloth, and on the cloth he poured powders from two or three jars. He was a famous pill-maker. He would never tell what ingredients he used for his medicines, but people came to him from all over the colliery for cures.

Even Francis's father would admit that they were a sight better than the bottle you got from the doctor, or even any patent medicine you could buy. Whatever opinion he had of the old man's religion, he had the greatest respect for his pills.

The old man bent over the powders, softening and mixing them. Then he very carefully rolled the mixture between his fingers until he had made a dozen little black pills, as round as beads. Then after he had dusted them with icing-sugar, he put them in a screw of clean paper, and made Francis put them carefully in his safest pocket.

'There now,' he said. 'Now for a breath of fresh air before rest. I always like to feel the wind on my face for a few minutes before I go to bed.'

He stood up, put on his hat and reached for his stick. He was a small man, but he was still straight and looked as tough and unbreakable as his stick. Once he had told Francis the strange story of his birth. 'I didn't come into this world alone, Francis,' he said. 'No, God sent me into this world with a marra. But my poor twin brother didn't live to see nine hours, and the Lord has seen fit to let me live for ninety years. My mother used to say that all the strength in that brother of mine went into me when he gave up the ghost. And sometimes I think she was right.'

Francis believed it. His grandfather was never ill, and never gave anyone trouble. His daughters had begged him over and over again to come and live with them, but he was proud and fastidious. He had his own ways and would rather live alone and keep them than surrender them to live in greater comfort with others. Every morning he dipped his head into a bowl of clean water and opened his eyes under the water to cleanse them. Before and after every meal he gave thanks to God, no matter where he was. Every morning and evening, no matter what the weather, he went out into the fresh air, if only for a minute; and every night he read his chapter from the Bible.

'Are you coming down to see what's the matter with my da?' asked Francis when he saw him getting ready.

'No, I'm not. I've seen enough of them dirty colliery streets. I'm going to take my walk up the village and fill my lungs with good fresh air before I go to bed. Good night, my bonny lad, and don't forget to tell your father what I said about his bad ways.'

He was just about to turn away when out of the darkness appeared the figure of a man walking up the hill on the far side of the road. Francis did not recognize him, but his grandfather seemed to know who it was.

'Is that Michael?' he called out.

'Aye, that's me,' replied the man.

'Are ye off for a walk up the hill then?'

'Yes.'

'Just hold on then, Michael. I'll join you, as soon as I've seen my grandson off.'

'Who's that, Grandpa?'

'That's Michael Blamires and he's the sort of feller your father could take a few lessons from.'

'How's that, Grandpa?'

'You'll get to know in good time. Off you go, now, it's getting a bit late for a boy of your age to be out on the streets.'

As he turned to walk down the bank, Francis wondered what his grandfather meant, but he soon forgot about the strange man he had just seen, and began to think about his grandfather's habit of reading the Bible over and over again. Mr. Cresswell had once told them about a famous bridge that was so long that when the painters had come to the end it was time to start again at the beginning, and he thought how hateful it must be to have a job like that that never finished. He thought that some day he would like to read the Bible right through, just to say that he had done it. But he wouldn't keep on reading it.

Nor did he really believe that it was beer that gave his father a bad back. When he handed him the pills he did not add the advice.

9

A Visit to Newcastle

It was Saturday and the family was getting ready to go to Newcastle. Mr. Kirtley was walking about the house, looking for his braces and his studs, and pausing to trim his moustache in the mirror. As he went backwards and forwards he sang—

> ' I stand in a land of roses,
> But I dream of a land of snow,
> Where you and I were happy
> In the years of long ago . . .'

—then he would stop, not knowing what came next, and having to content himself with the tune alone. All his songs went like this. He began with great confidence, but he never got to the end of a song and had to start another.

> ' Speak ! speak ! speak to me, Thora,
> Speak from your Heaven to me . . .'

Again the words failed him, and he had to go on humming. Francis watched him, smiling at his queer ways. He liked to see him happy like this, with the week's work over and the prospect of a football match before him.

His father began to change into his serge suit. He unhooked his watch from his old waistcoat and put it on the kitchen table with the other things he had taken from his pocket. Lying beside the loose change and the watch there was a little copper disc that Francis had never seen before.

' What's this, da ? ' he asked.

' That—oh, that's my Jolly Boys badge. Dinna tak' a fancy to that, lad, or else I'll be in Queer Street.'

' What's the Jolly Boys, da ? '

' Oh it's just a bit of daftness. It's my badge. It shows I'm a paid-up member of the Jolly Boys.'

Francis burst out laughing. It was strange to think of his father as any kind of boy, let alone a Jolly Boy.

' Who are the Jolly Boys ? ' he asked.

' Oh there's about a dozen of us—Bill Ainslie, Mick Parkin, Toast Ord, Pompey Clennell and a few mair . . . Hewie Hewison and his brother. We've always been friends.'

' But what do you do ? '

' We have a drink together now and then. And sometimes we make up a party to see the races—at York and Catterick— if we can manage it.'

' Can anybody be a Jolly Boy ? '

' No, not anybody—just the dozen of us—friends and pals. Hey, Dot, do ye remember when we all used to wear the same ginger cap ? '

' That I do,' said his wife, ' and ye all looked a sight, that ye did.'

' Why, it was just a bit of fun. We've always been friends, so we clubbed togither once and got ourselves the same caps and had these badges made for the members. It was just daftness, Francis, but we had some nice times togither.'

' And did you all wear your ginger caps, da ? '

' When we went to the races, we did.'

' I bet you looked nice.'

' They were as daft as brushes, the lot of them,' said his wife.

' It was just a bit of fun. We all started in the pit about the same time. We were putters togither and then hewers togither. We've always stuck togither—like the folks of Shields, as they say.'

' Don't you go to the races now, da ? '

' No, not so much nowadays.'

' Why not ? '

' L.s.d., my lad. Spondulix. There's not as many of the John

Bradburys as there used to be just after the war. Pocket-money's
not as plentiful as it used to be in them days.'

'But you'll still keep belonging to the Jolly Boys, won't you,
da?'

'As lang as I can. Just watch my little medal there, and see
that it doesn't get lost. The Jolly Boys are still hanging together.
We're not finished yet—not quite.'

He wandered off, looking for a brush to give his best boots a
lick, and starting optimistically on one more song—

> ' Give me your smile, the love-light in your eyes,
> Life could not hold a fairer Paradise!
> Give me the right . . .'

Francis was excited. His father had taken one look at the

paynote the night before and made up his mind to take the family to Newcastle to see the football match—at least Francis and he were to see the game, and Mrs. Kirtley was to meet them, as she always did, under the clock in the covered market; and old Mr. Pybus who lived at the end of the street had asked Francis when he knew where he was going to take one of his pigeons with him, and let it off at half-time with a message telling the score.

The family parted company at the Central Station in Newcastle, and as soon as Simon had left his wife, an extraordinary impatience came over him. Francis had never seen him walk so fast. They dodged in and out of the crowds, overtaking man after man, and dived down short cuts as if the whole world were competing for seats; but the more they overtook the more there were still ahead of them, and the queue for the turnstile was long. This was the one thing about going to St. James's that Francis did not like. As he pushed in after his father he held the little bag with the pigeon high about his head, and did not feel easy until the great iron arm had swung away before him.

Then his father ran clattering up the stone gangway, and at last they came to the top and saw the great hollow of the stadium, vast and green before them. They shuffled along the rows of the stand until they found good seats. Then Mr. Kirtley relaxed and opened his programme; but Francis had eyes only for the vast crowd, the tiers of faces rising on the terraces until the topmost row was outlined against the sky, the policemen and ambulance men patrolling the touchlines, the sellers of chewing-gum and chocolate throwing their packages dexterously up into the crowd and catching the coins as they were pitched down to them. He sat on the bench with the pigeon in his lap, looking at the far stand with its clock, whose fingers never seemed to move. There was nothing he hated more than waiting for those pointers to go round, and nothing he enjoyed more than that marvellous moment when the crowd began to roar and the trim players, jogging up and down to flex their muscles, came running out of the tunnel, and the referee had finished testing the nets and had blown up the two captains to begin the game. From then on he could not bear to lose one kick, one movement, one moment of the game.

As soon as the first half was over he took the pigeon out, slipped a note with the score inside the ring, and threw the bird up into the air. It clapped its wings noisily, then flew out into the free air above the pitch, and began to circle the field—once, twice—and then made off deliberately and quickly until it disappeared beyond the heads of the spectators.

The game came to an end all too quickly. While the ground staff were taking up the flagposts, Francis and his father shuffled along between the seats, kicking the cigarette ends and treading on the flattened packets. Beyond the turnstiles the crowds thinned away sadly.

Mr. and Mrs. Kirtley always arranged to meet after the game at the same place—under the clock in the covered market. They were all on time, and after they had had tea, Francis's father took him down a dark little street near the market where men were selling dogs. They never bought one. His mother was no lover of animals and would not have a dog or a cat in the house. But Francis liked to look at the puppies, to file slowly past the men with the dogs wrapped in their jackets so that all you could see was the dark velvet muzzles peeping out. They made him wish he had a pet of his own, and set him thinking about the little blue hen that he had released at half-time. Where would it be now? Was it possible that with no power but its own wings and no knowledge but its instinct it had been able to find its way back to Hesleyside? He felt that he had to make sure that it had come home safely, and when they were back in Russell Street, and his mother was putting the sheet of paper over the blazer to brighten the almost dead fire, he slipped out to see Mr. Pybus.

'Did the little hen come back, Mr. Pybus?' he asked.

'Aye, she's back all right, Francis.'

'Was the message there?'

'Aye, it was there. And what was the final score then?'

But Francis hardly heard his question.

' Can I go and see it, Mr. Pybus ? '

' What, now ? '

' Yes, please.'

' Wait a bit then till I light the muggie.'

In the darkness they went out into the garden, and Mr. Pybus shone the lamp into the cree; and there, sitting on its nest, blinking at the unaccustomed light, but composed and undistressed, sat the little hen.

There was something about the achievement of the bird that filled Francis with admiration, and it was shortly after he had looked into the cree and seen it, with all the hazards of its journey behind it, looking at him with no trace of resentment or fatigue in its bright shining eye, that he began to dream that he, too, could fly. In a still and empty world he would suddenly rise from the ground, and, using his arms like wings, go soaring and sweeping through the air. It was a miraculous feat that filled his sleep with triumph, and, night after night, he dreamt that he was riding high like a bird, traversing with an easy motion the slatey roofs of the colliery rows with their black chimneys. It was sad to wake and find himself earthbound and immobile in his bed, but the warmth and softness of the bedclothes took the bitterness from his waking, and he sank back into sleep with the memory of his miraculous flight flooding his spirit with tranquillity.

10

Armistice Day and a Quarrel

ONLY a few weeks after the famous battle of the Broom the time came round to commemorate another greater victory. On November 11th the Headmaster assembled the whole school to remember all those who had died for King and Country in the Great War.

This was the third time he had called the school together to give thanks for the defeat of the Germans, and the second time he had called for two minutes' silence. The partitions were all thrown back, and the whole school, even the Infants, were massed around the dais on which his desk stood. They were assembled in good time for the ceremony so that he could have time to remind them of its meaning. This time he began by holding up two or three medals, turning them to right and left so that all the pupils could see them.

' Can you all see these ? ' he said. ' They're medals. They're the kind of medals that have been issued to all the gallant soldiers who fought for us in the Great War. The war that ended on this day and at this time two years ago. Those who can wear them are lucky men, because many of our brave soldiers never came back. They made the supreme sacrifice, and today all the country, not just Hesleyside school, is remembering the men who fell. What I want you to do—and that means you, Christopher Ord, and you, Enoch Howden—is to stand quite still for two minutes and think of those men. When I've finished talking to you, you'll hear the colliery buzzer. That's the sign that the two minutes' silence is beginning. Don't just stand and think of nothing, but say a prayer—to yourselves—for all the British soldiers who gave their lives for King and Country and Empire. Is that clock right, Mr. Hall ? '

'Yes, sir, it's been checked.'

'Right. Now there'll be two buzzers, one to tell you when to start and another to tell you when the silence is over. And don't think once it's over that you can all start talking again. Just close your eyes and keep quiet until I tell you what to do next.'

A silence fell over the school, and a few moments later they heard the first buzzer. Francis closed his eyes and tried to think as he had been instructed, but he could not concentrate, not even on the memory of his uncles who had been killed in France. He found the silence and the stillness almost unbearable. He began to count to himself, but even after he had come to 120 the second buzzer had not blown. He opened his eyes a little, and saw the Headmaster glowering at the boys and girls in front of him as if he were more concerned with spotting offenders than in remembering the dead. The silence lengthened and lengthened until he was afraid that he would move and knock something and disturb it; but at last the buzzer sounded, and he could hear the whole school stirring and sighing with relief that the enforced and unnatural silence was over.

'Right,' said the Headmaster. 'I hope you all honoured the fallen as you were supposed to. Now you can go out to play. But don't think just because it's Armistice Day that you're going to get an extension. We're here to work, even though it is Remembrance Day. Lead them out, Mr. Hall.'

Last year the teacher who had taken them after the ceremony had told them to put away their books and had talked to them about the war. Francis hoped that Mr. Cresswell might do the same, but he was disappointed. Mr. Cresswell seemed in no mood to indulge them. He made them take out their Bibles and turn to the Acts of the Apostles.

There was no more talk of the war for the rest of the day.

But that night Francis asked his uncle Thomas if he had any medals like the ones the Headmaster had shown them. Thomas went up to the attic and brought down two, each with brightly coloured ribbons to them.

' Why don't you wear them, Uncle Thomas ? You can wear them, can't you ? '

' Oh, they're just for show, Francis. It's all right if you go in processions and things like that, but I dinna bother with them.'

' I think they want brightening up a bit. Look, they've gone dull. Shall I give them a polish ? '

' If tha likes. But I never take them out from one year to another.'

Francis was a bit disappointed that his uncle showed so little interest in his medals. He polished them with Brasso, and made Thomas pin them on his coat, but his uncle did not keep them there for long. Taking them off and putting them aside he began to talk of something else.

The following Sunday was Armistice Sunday and the papers were full of the celebrations, but neither his father nor his mother seemed very interested. Mr. Kirtley went off to the Club as usual for his Sunday morning drink, and as soon as dinner was over he picked up the paper and took himself off for his Sunday afternoon nap.

Mrs. Kirtley finished the washing-up and settled down in the rocking-chair with her feet on the fender. ' Don't forget to wait for your Grandpa when you come out of Sunday School,' she said. ' He's coming to have his tea with us today. And he likes it at five prompt so that he can get to Chapel in good time. So don't go wandering off, mind. I don't like to keep him waiting, so don't go straying off somewhere where you can't be found.'

Francis's grandfather was the Superintendent of the Methodist Sunday School. He was the one who heard the children say their Golden Texts, the verses they had to try to memorize. Francis always got the text by heart, partly to please his grand-father, and partly because at the end of the year there was a prize for the one who had recited the biggest number of texts. But it was a boring business listening to the same text over and over again, and he was glad when the recitations were over and it was time for the story. Generally they were about some very pious child who had behaved very righteously and shamed someone else who was a sinner, but this time his grandfather told them about an incident in the war, when the British soldiers had seen an angel in the sky and had taken heart and turned upon their enemies.

When the school was over he waited for his grandfather. The old man always went to look after the boilers to make sure they were stoked up in readiness for the evening service. Then they walked back together.

The table was ready for them. Although the old man was a sparing eater, his daughter always made a spread for him, with a bowl of pineapple chunks and a jug of Carnation cream. The old man did not care for chunks, but his daughter did not think that it was a proper Sunday tea without them.

When they were ready Francis called his father. He heard the bed creaking and the stairs squeaking as he got up. Sometimes, after a hard week, he would sleep on through tea-time, but he knew that the old man liked to see the family eating together. While they were waiting for Mr. Kirtley to come down, Grandpa washed his hands. He never ate without washing, and his daughter always set out a bowl of clean cold water and a clean towel for him. When he had finished he took his seat patiently at the table.

He was a very spruce old man. He sat bolt upright in his Sunday suit, with a clean handkerchief spread on his knees, and looked disapprovingly at his son-in-law, who sat down without washing or even putting on a collar and tie.

' Lad, I'm looking forward to a cup of tea,' said Mr. Kirtley. ' My mouth still feels full of coal-dust.'

He took a deep drink and then swept up the sides of his moustache in his swaggering way; but Francis saw that his grandfather had closed his eyes and was saying grace to himself as he always did.

' Well, where are ye off to today, Grandpa ? '

' I'm going where I always go on the Lord's Day—to the Lord's House—and it would be more to your credit if you were to get dressed and come with me.'

'Nay, Grandpa, it's not my line. It wouldn't do much good to a feller like me.'

'It would do you more good than sloping off to the Club, and filling yourself up with beer.'

'Every man to his own enjoyment, Grandpa. You go to your Chapel and your hymns, but I'd rather be supping a nice pint of Youngers.'

'It would be more fitting for you to be on your knees remembering—on this of all days—the poor men that were in the front line while you were at home.'

'I dinna forget them, Grandpa. I have one of them in my own house—and that's showing mair charity than many of the fellers that nivver remember them from one year's end to another. They'll be there, all right, to put the wreath on the memorial, but when it comes to finding a job for the poor lads that have come back wounded—aye, that's a different story.'

'Oh for heaven's sake,' said Mrs. Kirtley, 'don't let's have a quarrel. Not on this of all days.'

'I'm not quarrelling, Dot. But Grandpa can keep his service.'

'A godless man! A godless man! You always have been and you always will be!'

'I may be godless but I'm not a hypocrite. God nivver helped the poor miners and he nivver will. They'll have to help themselves in the future, 'cos naebody else will.'

'Now drop it, Simon. Come on now, get your tea, both of you.'

'I won't take another bite,' said the old man. 'I won't stay another minute in this house. You can insult me, Simon Kirtley, but I will not sit here and hear my Maker scandalized.'

'No, don't go, Grandpa. It's all a mistake. It's not worth having words about.'

But the old man would not be pacified. 'Give me my stick. When I hear the word of God insulted by my own relations, it's time for me to go.'

'Naebody's insulting your blessed religion, man,' said Simon. 'You stick to it, and good luck to you. But I'm telling you,

when the miners get into trouble again—and I can see it coming
—it's not the Chapel they'll turn to this time . . .'

But the old man had already taken his stick and gone, and
Francis sat looking at his father, wishing he had not lost his
temper. He hated to see his father and mother and grandfather
quarrelling like this, and wished he lived in a home where no one
argued. He took out the little leather-backed sketch-book that
his aunt had let him bring home, and wished again that he lived
in a big house where people did not argue but talked about
their travels and made drawings of the trees and the cows.

11

Sad News on a Sunday Night

MR. AND MRS. KIRTLEY said very little after the old man had gone. They were both vexed, Simon because he had lost his temper, and his wife because her father had been offended. Francis did not like to see them at loggerheads like this. He went for refuge to his cousin's house.

Happily there was no discord or conflict there. David was getting ready to go out to take part in a concert that the colliery band was giving. He was in his bandsman's uniform, and looked very smart and soldierly. To Francis he looked more enviable than ever with his long dark-blue trousers trimmed with scarlet braid, and his close-buttoned military jacket. He was a fine-looking boy, far taller than Francis with fair hair that lay close and neat on his head. Francis had tough black hair that stuck up like a brush at the back and would never lie flat. Elizabeth adored her son, and at times like these, when her house was not troubled by the noisy, common presence of her husband, her admiration shone out from her face. She was a good-looking woman, with slight, refined features and pretty ear-rings. There was a strain of good looks in the family that she and her son had inherited but neither Francis nor his mother possessed.

When David had gone Francis told her about the quarrel.

' Oh, don't worry about that,' she said. ' Your father and grandfather fight like cat and dog. They always have. But your father never holds a grudge against anybody. Just you watch, pet. It'll all blow over. I bet they've forgotten all about it by supper-time.'

It seemed as if she was right. When Francis went home he found the house full of company—Mrs. Ord and Mrs. Ainslie and one or two other wives of his father's friends who often came together on Sunday evenings when their husbands were at the Club. They all looked neat in their best clothes and white aprons.

He sat down in a corner and began to listen to their gossip. He liked hearing them talk. Their easy unquarrelsome ways were warm and comforting after the bickering of tea-time. They laughed often, throwing their aprons over their faces at something especially funny, as if they did not want to show how much they were amused. Then, knowing that the men would come soon and there would be too many of them to sit around the table, they had their supper and cleared the table and made it ready for their husbands.

Just after ten they heard the noise of boots coming over the yard, and the door swung open.

' Here they come, the Jolly Boys,' said one of the women.

' Aye, that's us, Lilah,' said Mr. Kirtley. His face was red with drinking and the walk home. ' We're the boys that make no noise.'

' It would take something to keep you quiet once you've had a drop inside you. I bet you've all had a skinful.'

' Nay, you couldn't drown a lop in what we've had, Lilah.'

' Aye and the rest ! '

' Come on,' said Mrs. Kirtley. ' Sit yourselves down and reach to. And ye canna blame us if there's not much left.'

She spoke jokingly. She would have been ashamed if there had not been a good spread for the men, for Sunday supper was one of the great feasts of the week, and there would be nothing to equal it till another week-end came round. The cold meat was heaped on the plates, the big pan sizzled with frying potatoes and carrots and cabbage, and the table was loaded with bread and butter, scones and teacakes, tarts and beetroot and bottles of sauce. The men ate heartily, and when the women had cleared away, sat round the table smoking.

' Come on, then, Toast,' said Mr. Kirtley. ' Give us a song to finish with. Give us " The Grey-Headed Miner ", Toast.'

' Nay, I canna sing that, Simon.'

'What? Naebody sings it the way thoo dis. Come on now, order for Toast and his song!'

The women stilled their gossip, and without getting up from his seat Mr. Ord tilted his head back a little, fixed his eyes on the clock on the far wall, and began to sing in a queer droning voice—

> ''Twas in the month of December
> On the banks of the Deerness,
> I saw an old miner
> Who was deep in distress.
> His brow was all wrinkled and
> His hair had turned grey.
> As I sat down beside him
> To me he did say,
> "Now I'm an old miner
> Aged fifty and six.
> If I could get lots, lads,
> I'd raffle my picks.
> Aye, or else I would sell them
> Or give them away,
> I can't get employment,
> For my hair has turned grey."'

They all listened carefully, but Mr. Ord had just come to the end of the first verse when Francis heard another voice calling out in the darkness of the street outside.

'Listen, da,' he said. 'I think it's the caller.'

'Nay, hinny, I dinna think it can be the caller at this time of night. Give us the next verse, Toast.'

Mr. Ord started on the second verse, but he had sung no more than a few lines when he began to falter.

'I think the lad's reet, Simon. Listen.'

They all fell silent and from the darkness of the street came the drawn-out, melancholy voice of the caller.

> 'All pits idle th'morn.
> All pits idle th'morn.'

' That's the first time I've ever heard the caller come round on a Sunday night. That's a fine start to the week,' said Francis's father. He looked a little puzzled.

' What are they idle for ? ' asked one of the women.

' God knows, Sarah,' said Mr. Kirtley. ' Naebody seems to want any coal nowadays. They say they can't sell it. Well, there's another shift gone west.'

Francis looked in bewilderment from face to face. He had expected to see them glad that they had not to go to work, that they could be on holiday. But the men did not looked pleased. A look of disappointment and anxiety came into every face, and they all forgot that Mr. Ord had not finished his song.

12

No Jobs For Heroes

THE war had now been over for more than two years. For the people of Hesleyside they had been years of dwindling prosperity. At first there had been no shortage of work and the men had drawn good wages. With Mr. Kirtley's pay and the little that Thomas paid for his board there was money enough in the household for them to live comfortably. But little by little the post-war boom began to fade and slacken, and day after day the caller was heard going from street to street with the melancholy tidings that the pit was to be idle for one more day. More and more days were lost and everyone began to feel the pinch. For the Kirtleys there were fewer visits to Newcastle, and less luxuries at the week-end. There was news, too, of differences between the owners and the men, and talk of reductions in wages. It seemed as if the world no longer needed either coal or the men that mined it.

It seemed, too, as if the spirit that had bound people together in the war years and the years following the Armistice was fading. Just after the war, when Thomas had come to stay with the Kirtleys, Francis made a surprising discovery about him.

' Is that Mr. Cresswell that teaches you called Percy Cresswell ? ' his uncle asked one day.

' Yes. I've heard the other teachers calling him Percy. Do you know him, Uncle Thomas ? '

' I should think I do. We were in the D.L.I.'s together—the Durham Light Infantry. He was a prisoner with me for a lang time.'

' Was he a prisoner of war as well ? '

' I should think he was. Ask him next time you speak to him if he remembers Tommy Hewitt.'

When he got a chance Francis mentioned his uncle's name to Mr. Cresswell.

'Thomas Hewitt? Of course I know him. How is he now? Is he working again?'

'Yes, Mr. Cresswell.'

'So he's your uncle, is he?'

'Yes, sir.'

It made him feel proud and important to have an uncle who was the friend of a teacher.

'Well, just you tell him, Kirtley, that any time he would like to come and see me and have a chat about old times I'll be pleased to see him. Tell him he'll be very welcome.'

Francis passed on the message, but to his surprise, although his uncle kept on sending messages from time to time to his war-time friend, he never went to see him, and always found an excuse for putting off his visit. It was as if he knew that they could never be friends again as they had been in the P.O.W. camp. Once they had been fellow soldiers, but now one of them was a miner again, and the other a teacher. The bond that had once linked was now parting. The messages grew less and less frequent, then ended altogether. The comradeship was over, and both seemed to forget that they had ever been friends.

As the times worsened, Mr. Kirtley grew puzzled and irritable. He did not take kindly to being short of money, but what disturbed him most was his inability to understand what was happening to him and his fellows. He was filled with a sense of betrayal and confusion, unable to understand how it was that the pit was idle day after day, and ready to hit out at anyone who might be considered responsible for the failure of the coal trade.

One day when Francis was looking for a book in a cupboard in the ' room ', he came across a gramophone that his father had bought in the good days just after 1918. It had a dull green horn that looked like a partly folded umbrella, a rusted handle and a sound-head like a big old-fashioned watch. Once they had used it a great deal and Francis remembered one song that his father had been very fond of. It was called ' When Father Papered the

Parlour '. That record seemed to be missing now, but in the lid of the gramophone there were two or three others, mainly of war songs—' Tipperary ', ' There's a Silver Lining ', ' The Roses are Blooming in Picardy '—songs that Francis could remember people singing when the war was on.

Once they used to enjoy playing the gramophone, but lately they had all lost interest in it. They had not bought any new records for a long time, and the gramophone had been stored away in the cupboard.

Francis thought he would like to hear one of the records again. He took out the gramophone and wound it up with its rusty handle, and picked a record, ' Carry Me Back to Dear Old Blighty '; but as he was trying to put the record on, it slipped through his fingers and broke.

It would have been easy to conceal the accident, but Francis had a fear of being what his mother called ' underhand '. Although he could sense that his father was in a bad mood, he took the broken record to him.

' I'm sorry, da,' he said, ' but I broke this record when you were at the pit.'

' Which one is it ? '

' It's the one about Blighty.'

He held out the part of the record that had the title on it.

' Blighty, eh ? Well, tha needn't lose any sleep about that. Blighty—aye, and a damn fine place it is ! Here—give it to me.'

He took the record and flung the pieces on to the fire.

' That's the best place for it ! '

' Don't you like the song, da ? '

' Like it ? I mortally hate it. I'm sick of the war and all the misery it's fetched to this place. I don't want to hear any mair about it. Are there any other records like that one ? '

' I think there's a few.'

' Chuck the lot on the fire—no, I'll chuck them on mysel' 'cos that's all they deserve.'

He went angrily into the ' room ', came out with his hands full of records and pitched them violently into the grate.

' That's what I think about them!' he shouted, and taking the poker, he began to batter them until they broke into little pieces that melted and oozed away.

' That's the end of them—and a good riddance,' he shouted. ' The flaming war—I never want to hear another word about it —'cos it's brought nowt but trouble and misery to ivvery man in this colliery.'

The next day Francis understood why his father had been in such a fury. His uncle Thomas, and two or three others who had come back wounded from the war, and had all been given light jobs, had been given notice. There was no more work for them in Hesleyside.

Thomas stayed on at Russell Street, dependent, and deeply ashamed of having to sponge on his brother-in-law; but Mr. Kirtley would not hear of his leaving. ' As long as I've a home, it's thine as well, Tommy,' he said. ' Tha'll get another job somewhere. Time enough to think of leaving us when tha's compelled to.'

Thomas tried to help in the house, but there was little he could do, and time hung heavily on his hands. He would sit despondently in the house until out of pity his sister gave him the price of a drink and entry into the Club where he could spend an hour or two in happy company. Once after he had won a few shillings on a coupon, he let himself go and had too much to drink.

Francis was still up when he came in. He had a happy but foolish look on his face, like a child that wanted to break out laughing but knew it had to behave itself. He was holding himself stiffly upright, as if he were confusing the house with a guardroom and wanted to conceal the fact that he had drunk too much, but when he began to pull off his jacket his hands would not do what he wanted them to do.

' It doesn't take much to see where you've been,' said Mrs. Kirtley sarcastically.

' I've had a drop, Dot,' he said. ' I'll not deny it, I've had a drop.'

' Yes and mair than a drop, if you ask me.'

She had her father's hatred of drunkenness and made no attempt to hide her disgust.

' I'll be nae trouble, Dot,' said Thomas, drawing himself up even more stiffly. ' I can look after myself.'

' And what about your supper ? '

' Never mind about that. I'll just take myself off to bed.'

' And that's the best place for anybody in your condition.'

' I'm not drunk. I can take care of myself.'

He sat down and took off his boots, his hands fumbling at the laces. Then very gravely and stiffly he went upstairs and they heard the sound of his attic door closing.

' I hope he's not going to start that game,' said Mrs. Kirtley.

' Dinna begrudge the lad a few drinks. It's not ivvery day he gets the chance of a drop. He's had a lot to put up with, and there's not much of a prospect in front of him.'

But his wife was not prepared to be as tolerant. She began to rake over the coal in sharp, angry movements, and when she told Francis to get to bed there was a note in her voice that he did not dare disobey.

A few weeks later Thomas found a job, but it was not in Hesleyside or anywhere near it. It was in Saltburn and taking it meant leaving the place where he had been born and spent most of his working life. But there was no option for him. He packed his things and said good-bye.

It was just after he had gone that Mrs. Kirtley, going through the ' room ', came across the gramophone that had never been played since the day when Francis broke the record. Now the spring was broken and the turntable would not spin so she took it upstairs and dumped it in the attic where Thomas had slept, where it stood gathering dust alongside the other souvenirs of the poor unwanted soldier who had been driven to seek new work among strangers. Occasionally Francis, rummaging among the junk in the abandoned room, would pick up the horn and blow through it, but the only sound he could get from it was a forlorn and lugubrious note that filled the untenanted attic.

13

The Gun

ALTHOUGH most of the men in Hesleyside wanted to forget the war and all its consequences, there were others who seemed bent on reminding them of it. Just before Easter the news went round that the Council had accepted the offer of a captured German field-gun and were planning to set it up on a piece of waste ground between the colliery pond and the pit offices. They were not the only Council to do this. Many had been given captured guns or tanks and had put them up as a kind of second war memorial or a victory trophy. The tanks that Francis had seen in Durham were still there. But the men of Hesleyside were in an angry mood. The victory over the Germans had brought neither prosperity nor happiness to them, and they were in no mood to rejoice over a triumph that to them was taking on the look of a miserable defeat.

Mr. Kirtley was among the men who felt that the proposal was an insult to the colliery, and Francis heard him often talking about it.

' There'll be ructions about that gun, Dot. Have you heard the latest ? '

' No.'

' Some of the lads have sent a deputation to the Council telling them just what they think.'

' And what did the Council say ? '

' Just what you'd expect them to say. They've spent money fetching it and they're not going to spend mair having it carted away.'

' But they'll spend money putting it up.'

' They've started concreting the base already.'

' Fancy spending on a thing like that, with all the things that want doing here.'

' Aye it would have been mair menseful if they'd tried to find a job for lads like your Thomas, for instance. It makes my blood boil, Dot, when I think of the shameful way them lads have been treated. They gave four of the best years of their lives in the trenches, and now they canna get a day's work. Now they're wasting good money on things like this gun. The flaming hypocrites! They'll get a sneck afore their snouts if they carry on with this.'

' Well, just take care, Simon, and don't do anything rash. We canna afford to get into trouble just now. Things are bad enough without that.'

Francis looked up from time to time to listen to the conversation, only half understanding his father's anger. He was reading an encyclopaedia that his mother had bought for him some time ago. It wasn't a proper encyclopaedia. It was called *Cassell's Book of Knowledge*. There ought to have been eight volumes of it, but Mrs. Kirtley had found it hard to keep up the instalments and the last two volumes had never been bought.

Incomplete though they were, these books were a great source of pleasure to Francis. He loved the pictures of foreign lands and the ingenious diagrams of the human body revealing the coiled organs and the weird process of eating and digesting. But most of all he loved to read about ancient civilizations, to calculate over and over again how many centuries ago it was when the Greeks had built their temples and the Babylonians their ziggurats, and the Egyptians had buried their mummified kings in their pyramids. His mind roved deeper and deeper into the past with an unsatisfied craving, seeking for accounts of even earlier civilizations. He came across mention of another people called the Sumerians, but the sixth Book of Knowledge ended at SCA, and he could not read about them as he wanted to. Somewhere, too, he had heard about a mysterious castle in Africa called by the enticing name of Zimbabwe, but alas that, too, came in the missing later books. He had to be content to let his imagination play upon the images of these vanished peoples and their works. He let it range more and more deeply into the past until a kind of dizziness came over him, as if he were being transported bodily over great gulfs of time, and his body like his mind were reeling in the act of reaching farther and farther backwards into the past.

At school, too, he began to devour knowledge with a great and growing appetite. He had taken a second examination for the Grammar School. Apparently the errors of his first answers had been forgiven after all, and he was among those chosen to attempt the second hurdle. This time he kept his head and looked closely at the instructions.

In addition a new venture was opening before him. Nobody in Hesleyside had ever studied a foreign language before, but a new teacher came to the school, and the Headmaster had given him permission to start French lessons with some of the top classes. Francis picked it up quickly. It made him proud to be mastering something that no one in Hesleyside had done before him.

Best of all he loved the French songs that Mr. Curry taught them. His favourite was one which began:

> *J'avais un camarade*
> *Le meilleur d'ici bas* . . .

He had always loved singing, and to be able to sing in a foreign language gave him great pleasure. It was not just the sensation of being able to understand another tongue; it was almost as if he became another person. When he sang his favourite song he knew that he was singing about his dear cousin, David, his ' *camarade—Le meilleur d'ici bas* '. The song had a sad ending, but he hardly noticed that. It was enough that it helped him to voice something nothing else could express for him.

He took a great delight in French phrases, and once when he was writing an English essay on Joan of Arc he gave her her French name, ' Jeanne d'Arc '. His father was a bit uneasy when he read the essay and came to the unfamiliar spelling.

'Surely, bonny lad, that's not the way to spell her name, is it? Tha's made a bit of a slip there.'

'No, I haven't, da,' he said. 'That's the French way.'

'Why, just watch tha dissent get ower clivver, Franky. Dinna get ower sharp or else tha'll be cutting thissel.'

But Francis knew that he was right, although he was sorry he had sounded conceited over it.

Something in him seemed to be waking. Almost everything he saw, smelt, heard and touched interested him, but best of all he liked those things that came to him with an unexpected sense of mystery, like the sounds of the cathedral bells travelling over the still land on a quiet night, the sudden flashing of a shooting star, the sound of the bandsmen at their practice in the little room on the edge of the colliery, even the crowding and mysterious shapes of houses and trees as he walked home in the dark. No one else seemed to hear and see these things, but they entered into him and remained part of him.

It was not easy for him to be concerned about the problems that were beginning to disturb his father; but one day when he was going to the Broom for his mother, he saw something that reminded him of the angry conversation he had half-heard when he had been reading his encyclopaedia. It was the gun. It had arrived, and was sitting squarely on the block of concrete that had been prepared for it, shackled like a captured animal, with its muzzle pointing upwards defiantly, as if it were about to emit some ugly and menacing cry.

Hesleyside Wins the Cup

ALTHOUGH Francis never forgot how kind Mr. Cresswell had been to him during the examination, he remained a little afraid of him, and the departure of his uncle, who had been, for a while at least, a link between teacher and pupil, made Mr. Cresswell even more remote and distant. It was in his nature to be aloof and inaccessible, but he had done a great deal for Hesleyside. In particular he had given the school a football team that the whole colliery was proud of. Before Mr. Cresswell came, there had been no field, no goalposts, no balls, no players. Somehow he had managed to provide all these things, and had trained a side that was among the best in the county. Everyone spoke highly of him, for they knew that without him the team would never have come into being, let alone make a name for itself.

Still Francis was a little afraid of him. He was a good teacher, but he had little patience with duffers, and sometimes he lost his temper with the whole class.

One day his father told him something that helped him to understand Mr. Cresswell. When Francis was telling how bad-tempered the teacher had been, his father said, 'I can understand the poor fellow being on edge, Francis. He's had a big disappointment in his life.'

'What was that?'

'Why he was a footballer hisself afore the war. One of the best, they say.'

'A real footballer?'

'Toast Ord says he was on Chelsea's books. I nivver saw him play, but they say he was one of the best young players Chelsea had. And a good prospect for an England cap.'

'Why didn't he get one?'

' The same old story, Francis. He copped a bad wound in the arm and another in the leg.'

' Is that why his arm's bent ? '

' That's it.'

' But he doesn't limp like Uncle Thomas did.'

' Maybe not. But them wounds and three years in the prisoner-of-war camp—they put the kibosh on his career. Poor lad. He might have been a real top-notcher if it hadn't been for the war.'

Francis could see now why Mr. Cresswell was so often disappointed and bad-tempered. The next time he took them for a lesson, Francis looked closely at him to see if he limped. He could see no signs of it, but when he told David what his father had told him, his cousin said it was true. After this Francis looked at Mr. Cresswell with new respect, all the more because, whatever triumphs and disappointments this stern young man might have lived through, he never spoke of them but kept them all locked away in his proud heart.

Under his guidance the Hesleyside boys had had a season of great triumphs, and the people had taken the team to their hearts. Perhaps because they had now less money to go and see the great first league teams, perhaps because Hesleyside had never before had any claim to distinction of any sort, the folk of the colliery thronged to support the boys. Now, as the season was coming to its climax, they had fought their way through to the final of the County Schools Cup against Tadfield, a big colliery on the far side of the county.

On the Saturday of the game Hesleyside looked like an abandoned village. Almost every man, woman and child had gone, by train or on foot, to the Hollow Drift field in Durham where the final was to be played. Among the few left at home were David's father and mother, he out of his incurable cussedness, she because she could not bear to see her boy in danger of being hurt.

Francis went, as always, with his father. They walked the four miles into the city, planning to come home by train when the game was over. They got there early and walked around the field.

It was a beautiful field, very smooth and level, unlike the bumpy and ridged Hesleyside field. The organizers had put up two tents for the teams to change in. Francis wanted to go in to see if he could speak to David, but the man at the door turned him away. All he could do was to peep in, smell the exciting smell of trodden grass and see the boys changing into their green-and-white shirts. It was still half an hour before kick-off, so they wandered round the field looking for the best place.

When at last they took their places, it seemed as if the ground was full of unfamiliar faces, men, women and boys flaunting enemy colours, calling out to one another in an accent almost as strange as the language of foreigners. Hesleyside had almost emptied itself for the game, but even then they were greatly

outnumbered. Tadfield was a far bigger colliery than the Side, and its supporters' red-and-white favours were everywhere; the roar of their acclamation as the boys ran on to the field made the Hesleyside welcome sound thin.

'By sangs,' said Mr. Kirtley, ' these lads will take some beating. They have some beef on them, haven't they?'

At first it looked as if Mr. Kirtley's fears were well-founded. Within a quarter of an hour the Tadfield boys were in the lead. Flushed with this success they attacked again and again, and with every surge on the Hesley-side goal their supporters grew more and more jubilant. Looking round anxiously, Francis seemed to see nothing but Tadfield men, twirling their painted crakes and waving their red-and-white scarves. But the Hesleyside boys had been well-trained, and, as if something of Mr. Cresswell's fortitude had entered into them, they held their ground. Then just before half-time, Pompey Ramsay, the clever little centre-forward who had scored so often for them in the earlier rounds, broke through the Tadfield defence and forced his way close to the goal. Before he could shoot he was brought down from behind by a savage tackle, and the referee blew and pointed to the penalty spot.

At once a wild howl of protest was heard from every part of the field, and two women ducked under the ropes not far from where Francis and his father were standing and ran on to the field. The referee did not seem to notice them, so busy was he ordering the field so that the kick could be taken. Before he knew what was happening one of the women seized him from behind and pulled so hard at him that Francis could hear the cloth of his light jacket being ripped. When he turned round she struck at him in her rage with her umbrella. He ducked to avoid the blow, but it caught him on the shoulder and knocked him down, and the second woman ran at him as if she meant to tread on him. But by now the two linesmen had come to his help, and behind them the rest of the spectators. They swarmed round the fallen referee like bees and a dozen fights broke out. Francis saw one man felled with a blow on the jaw, and his assailant in turn seized from behind and thrown down. The game had suddenly been transformed into an angry mêlée with men and women struggling to get at the referee or his assailants, the wilder hitting out in all directions and the more sensible trying to keep enemies apart. Men and women and boys all seemed involved in the brawl that neither officials nor policemen could end.

In all this no one touched or even spoke to the players. They stood unhappily in two groups on the fringe of the milling crowd, bewildered by what had happened, not knowing what to do, a little guilty that it was their play that had precipitated this unexpected and ugly scene.

Then, as suddenly as it had been invaded, the field began to clear. The women were led away weeping and protesting, men who had seemed enemies a moment before ran off side by side, and nothing was left but a small knot of men around the injured referee. Too hurt to carry on, he was helped away. One of the linesmen took his whistle, and put the ball on the penalty spot. In a deep silence David walked calmly up to the ball and kicked it carefully into the net. Before the game could restart, the referee blew his whistle for half-time.

This was the turning point in the game. As soon as play was resumed it was easy to see which of the two teams had been the more upset by the bad behaviour of the crowd. The Tadfield boys, no longer in the lead, began to play wildly as if their confidence had been taken from them by the unruliness of their supporters. In contrast, the boys of the Side seemed steadied and confident. When they scored their second goal, Francis expected another demonstration, but the Tadfield folk, as if stunned by the unexpected turn of the game, were silent. It was as if all their pent-up passions had been dissipated by their wild outburst, and all they could do was to stand and watch the inevitable defeat of their team.

It was David who completed their downfall. All who saw the game said afterwards that they had never seen a schoolboy play with such mastery. He commanded the middle of the field like a true captain, robbing the Tadfield forwards again and again, and sending his own forwards away with swift passes that bewildered their opponents. In the end the Side had scored four goals and the cup was theirs.

By the time the cup had been presented and the speeches made and Francis and his father had made their way back to the station, the short Spring day was nearly over. Along the station platform the yellow gas-lamps had already been lit, with their little fish-tails of light hissing and rising and sinking as the draughts from outside blew in upon them. The platform was thronged with men, crowding around the cup, moving restlessly in and out of the pools of yellow light. They kept hoisting the cup, snatching it from one another, splashing beer into it and fighting to drink from it. Francis did not like to see them handling it so roughly. He saw Mr. Cresswell standing alone by the barrier, stern and undemonstrative. Men kept going up to him, insisting effusively on shaking his hand, pressing drunkenly against him and embarrassing him with their unwelcome invitations to him to drink. He looked aloof and displeased, anxious to be gone, but unwilling to depart until he had seen the precious cup safely on its way back to Hesleyside.

At last the train came in, backing fussily into the bay, the great glistening wheels turning slowly, and a cloud of smoke and steam billowing and writhing under the station roof. When it stopped, a man ran with the cup to the front of the train, trying to climb onto the footplate of the engine. The driver pushed him away with his foot and told him to get aboard. Then Francis heard the doors banging and saw the men struggling to get seats. The driver hooted impatiently, and soon there was no one left on the platform but Mr. Cresswell.

In the pale gaslight he looked vexed and ill. As the train began to pull out and he turned to go through the barrier, Francis saw him limping. It was the first time Francis had ever seen him show signs of the wound that his father had told him about.

On the Monday after the final the Headmaster kept all the school in the big hall after prayers.

' You all know what I want to talk to you about,' he said. ' Our boys have won the cup. Here it is and here it will stop till next year at least.'

He spoke as always in a rough, clipped manner that Francis did not like.

' You should all be proud of these boys. Here they are, all lined up for you. They've brought a lot of credit to the school and what I want you to do is give them three cheers.'

The school cheered as it had never cheered before. It was not often that they had the chance to make a noise like this in school and they made the most of it.

But the Headmaster had not yet finished. ' Now one of your

masters must get the credit as well. He's the one that's spent a lot of his time training the team. You know who it is. It's Mr. Cresswell. So three cheers now for him.'

The cheering broke out again. Francis thought that Mr. Cresswell might smile at the applause; but he looked as silent and aloof as he had on the station platform at Durham, looking glumly and stolidly before him as if he had not even heard what the Headmaster had said.

'Now then, there's another bit of news,' went on the Head. 'We've heard over the week-end that David Wilson has been given his county cap. So that's two honours for Hesleyside school. We've won the cup and for the first time in the history of the school one of our boys has been chosen for his county. So three more cheers now. This time for the team captain— David Wilson.'

For the third time the cheering rang out. But the Headmaster did not let it go on too long.

'That's enough now. We've wasted a lot of time this morning and we're here to work not to play. Lead on, Standard Seven. You've had a good week-end, but it's over now. Back to work everybody.'

The boys did not have much time to talk over the glorious events of the week-end, but Mr. Kirtley for one was still full of it.

'Well, I bet Mr. Cresswell was full of smiles today for once, was he, Frankie?' he asked when Francis came home. 'He'd be in a good mood for once, was he?'

'No, he wasn't. He put some terrible sums on the board and he was furious when we couldn't do them. I don't know what got into him.'

'I think I can guess.'

'What was it then?'

'Well, he didn't like the way the spectators behaved, for one thing.'

'But it wasn't us. It was the Tadfield folks.'

'We did our share—and it was just as bad the way the men went on at the Club.'

' What happened there ? '

' They behaved as if they'd nivver seen a cup afore—tossing it about as if it was a football—filling it up with beer. They dinna deserve to have a cup in their hands, some of them—tossing it about and dropping it on the floor. If it hadn't ha' been for the blacksmith it wad ha' been in a sorry state this morning. No, it wasn't good enough. I can understand Mr. Cresswell being vexed about it.'

' But the Headmaster didn't say anything.'

' Him—he wouldn't have noticed if there'd been a handle off.'

' Did one come off ? '

' Very nearly. Some of the men behaved just like hooligans. No, it wouldn't surprise me if Mr. Cresswell never entered another team.'

When Francis got a chance he took a close look at the cup. There didn't seem to be much wrong with it except that one of the handles looked a bit crooked, and perhaps one dent had been beaten out. But he didn't say anything to David about it. Rather than spoil his moment of triumph he would have kept a dozen secrets.

15

Hard Times

JUST after Easter the men were told that they would have to take lower wages. They refused and came out on strike. Francis was so absorbed in school and play that he hardly understood what the strike was about. There were some things about it that he did not like. A soup-kitchen was set up at the top of the colliery in a wooden hut and he begged his mother to let him go. But he soon regretted it. He didn't like the soup. It was not as thick as the broth his mother made, and the lettuce sandwiches he was given were tasteless. He hated the thick slices of bread thinly spread with margarine, but worst of all he hated the bossy old man who supervised the meals. He went round with a stick, yelling at the boys to get their elbows off the table and not to drink when they were eating. He was like one of those workhouse tyrants Francis had read about. He soon gave up going to the kitchen. He was glad to be at home again for his meals.

But the weather was good and the men, at first, made the most of it. Mr. Kirtley seemed ready to enjoy his holiday. He walked a great deal, and on occasions took Francis with him. He was a good companion; he knew much about the countryside and Francis liked to accompany him.

One day when they were passing the village they saw a short brick chimney that stood in a garden belonging to one of the few inhabited houses. It was too wide and short for an ordinary chimney, but not high enough to be called a tower. Francis had always wondered what it was, but he had never been able to explore it, nor did he know of any other boy who knew what it was for. The garden was owned by a bad-tempered old man who stopped the boys even from climbing on the wall, let alone going

over it. There were not many walls in the colliery that had not
been climbed, but the guardian of this one seemed determined
to prevent any boy from investigating the mystery in his garden.

But Mr. Kirtley knew what it was.

' It's an airshaft, Francis, that's what it is. A ventilation shaft.'

' What does it ventilate ? '

' I don't suppose it ventilates very much now, but it was put
up in the first place to let bad air out of the drifts.'

' Is there a drift under here ? '

' There are drifts ivverywhere in this place, hinny. The hill-
side is riddled with them.'

' Are there men still working under here ? '

' Not now. Most of the drifts are worked out. But this shaft
used to strike down to a drift where the air was bad.'

' Is it open then, like a pit shaft ? '

' Not now. They've boarded it up.'

' Are there any more of these ventilation shafts ? '

' There was a good few once. And I dare say you can still
come across one or two of them up on the fells. But mind, don't
you go playing about with them, because you could fall in and
nivver be seen again.'

The men enjoyed their freedom for a while, but they were not
used to idleness. They grew restless, and found work for themselves sorting out loose coal and coke on the Bleezer. They were
glad to be at work, using their muscles once more, even if only
to scavenge a little free house-coal.

When his father was changing into his pit clothes to go working on the Bleezer, Francis, hunting for a safety-pin for him, came
across something he had not seen for a long while. It was his
Jolly Boys badge.

' Hey, da, look what I've found.'

' What is it ? '

' It's your Jolly Boys badge.'

' Oh, that thing ! '

' What's the matter, da, don't you want it now ? Don't you
belong to the Jolly Boys any more ? '

' Naebody belangs to the Jolly Boys now, Frankie.'

' Why ? '

' We haven't the money we used to have. No, the Jolly Boys are disbanded, pet. Napoo, my boy, finished.'

' What should I do with the medal then ? '

' Chuck it away.'

' Don't you want to keep it ? '

' It's nae use to me or to anybody now. Hoy it on the fire.'

But Francis could not bring himself to do that. He put it in his pocket. Then one day when the boys were putting pins on the railway line to see what happened to them when the tankie ran over them, he remembered the disc and put it on the rail. He waited until the tankie and the trucks had all gone over it and ran to pick it up. It had been pressed into an uneven oval, and though the initials s o k were still legible, the letters j b on the other side had almost vanished.

The men were still out on strike, and everybody in the colliery was beginning to feel the pinch. The two missing volumes of the *Book of Knowledge* had still not been bought. When Francis asked his mother if she was going to get them for him she put him off.

' If we still had a bit of that money your father got when your Grandma Kirtley died I might have seen my way clear to get them, but there's not much in the kitty now, and it's all I can do to keep house and home together.'

Francis had hardly known Grandma Kirtley. She had died when he was very young, but one day he heard his father talking about her. Although she was only a miner's wife she had been very thrifty, and when she died all her children were astonished at what she had left them. Mr. Kirtley's share had gone long ago—in spending, in giving, in keeping his head above water in bad times. Like most of the people of Hesleyside he never saved. If he had money, he spent it ; if he had none, he did without. Nor had it ever occurred to Francis that he might be able to save for himself, but the story of his grandmother and her little hoard was a revelation to him, and he began to wonder if he could not do what she had done, and save enough money to buy the missing books for himself.

He began by shovelling coal for the women in the street. Their free loads of coal were dumped on the pavement and had to be moved, shovel by shovel, into the coal-house. It was hard work and he got no more than threepence a load, but he persisted and soon his savings amounted to a few shillings.

Then one day he found another job not quite so exhausting. There was an old woman in the next street who kept a fish-and-chip shop, and one day when he was going past her yard he saw her turning a clumsy old machine that she had bought for cleaning the potatoes. He offered to do the job for her, and to his surprise she took him on. Sometimes she wanted to pay him in fish and chips, but he stuck out for the money.

At last, with shovelling coal, cleaning potatoes and doing other odd jobs, he saved enough to pay for the last two volumes of the *Book of Knowledge*—SCA to VEM and VEN to ZYG. As soon as he had them in his hand he looked to see if there was anything about Zimbabwe. There was a long account, and reading it and looking at the pictures made up for all the blisters on his hands from shovel and handle.

16

The Long Walk

BEFORE the Easter holiday was over, Francis was sent off to spend a few days with his aunt Zillah who lived at Satley, a few miles from Tow Law. Holidays were a rare occurrence for the Kirtley family. When they were at work the men had only a day off here and there, at Christmas and on Bank Holidays; when they were on strike, they had no money for outings, except perhaps for the cheap trips run by the Sunday Schools. To spend a few days in a new house was a great treat and Francis looked forward to it.

But he had only been away for a few hours before he knew that he would not enjoy his stay. His uncle and aunt were elderly. Their sons and daughters were all grown up and married, and there was no one in the house for him to play with. He tried to join in with the Satley boys, but he found them hostile. They treated him like a spy or an enemy, and would not let him join in their games, making fun of the way he spoke and laughing at everything he did. He was driven back into the quiet childless house, where there was nothing for him to do but talk to his aunt.

He liked her. She was a fat, easy-going woman, kind and considerate, and she did her best to make the boy happy; but her husband was a rough old man, with horrible stiff whiskers and a sense of humour that Francis could not understand. His father had told him that the old man was very well off, and kept a store of sovereigns in his belt. He never parted with the belt and even slept in it. Francis saw the belt but he could not believe there were many sovereigns concealed in it. Perhaps his uncle was rich but to Francis he was only a rough old man with dirty habits and an unpleasant smell.

On the second night of Francis's stay his uncle came in from the pub, smelling strongly of beer, the bristles of his stiff beard glinting wickedly in the electric light.

'How's our little Francis getting on?' he shouted. He was a noisy man.

'Come on, lad, and I'll gie ye a scrub.'

Before Francis could escape, the old man seized him and began to rub his wiry beard against the boy's cheek. Francis struggled to get clear, but his uncle held him with his powerful hard arms, and rubbed his bristles against his face like a rasp.

'How dis tha like that, bonny lad? That'll give thee summat to talk about when tha gets home, eh?'

Francis broke away from him, smarting and feeling that the skin had been torn off his cheeks and chin. The rough, rasping whiskers and the beery smell of the old man made him feel sick and hurt.

But his uncle put back his head and laughed till the tears came into his watery eyes.

'What should we dee with him, Zillah?' he said. 'Tell ye what, we'll tie him on the back of the train and send him back to his mother, eh?'

'Give the bairn a bit of peace, Jack,' said his wife.

'I've got a nice lang rope in the shed,' he went on. 'We'll tie him behind the buffers. That's the best way of sending him back. He winna need a ticket if he travels that way.'

Francis was horrified. He backed away, but the old man kept up his dreadful laugh.

'What's the matter? Is tha frightened of thi uncle Jack, eh? Come on, I'll give tha another scrub.'

That night Francis had a nightmare. What had been to his uncle a joke, was to him a dreadful torture. He saw himself being dragged along at the tail of the train, his head bumping against the tarry sleepers, his skin being rasped and torn from his body by the rough cinders as it had almost been from his cheek by the wiry stubble of the old man's whiskers. His dream was so frightening that he awoke with a desperate longing to be home.

He wandered alone about the
streets, going back to his aunt's
only at meal-times; but after
tea the thought of having to
endure for one more evening
the wicked sport of his uncle
was too much for him. He
made up his mind to go home.
He had only the vaguest idea of
the distance that lay between
him and home but his craving
for the peace and security of his
mother's house was so over-
mastering that he never thought
of the dangers and hardships he
might have to face. He turned
his back upon the hated colliery
with its dirty yellow streets,
and walked away without stop-
ping to tell anyone what he
meant to do.

Once out of the colliery he saw nothing but fields with low,
scrubby hawthorn hedges, and dark grey sheep feeding on the
shabby grass. He was alone, but he was not afraid, for something
told him that this was the road he had to take and every step
was bringing him nearer to home. After an hour he passed
by the edge of a small colliery that he could not recognize,
with a high cable crossing the road on high pylons, and little
tubs going backwards and forwards over it, carrying slag to
a big tip in the field, and coming back dangling and empty.
Then, just beyond the cable, he saw a man sitting smoking by
the roadside.

'Please, is this the road to Hesleyside?' he asked the man.

'Hesleyside? Aye, ye can get to Hesleyside this way,' answered
the man. Francis was not afraid of him. He could see from his
clothes that he was a miner and not a tramp.

' But mind, it's a lang traipse,' the man went on. ' Are ye walking it ? '

' Yes.'

' Tha's got a good few miles in front of tha, hinny. What on earth are ye off to Hesleyside for ? '

' I'm going to see my mother.'

' She must be a queer mother to let her lad walk all this way by hissel. But carry on, hinny. This is the way. Mind it'll be dark afore ye get there.'

Francis hurried on. He was grateful for the help but he did not want to stay talking any longer in case the man asked him what he was doing, and made him go back. He walked on faster than ever. He was not tired. On the contrary he was buoyed up with a sense of wonder at finding himself in a strange country, and of triumph at being able to find his way across it. He looked forward to seeing his mother, to surprising her by his daring and enterprise.

But as mile after mile passed he began to feel concerned. He knew that sooner or later he would come to the beginning of Sandy Lonnen, a long, dusty lane that led over the fells to the high land on which Hesleyside village stood. But although he could see one or two familiar landmarks in the far distance, the buff walls of Ushaw College, and, even farther away, the prominent mound where Penshaw monument stood, he could not recognize the lonnen.

Besides it was now growing dark, and the stiff leather of his best shoes began to rub against the heel of his left foot, and gave him a blister. He sat down, took off shoe and sock and tried to prick the blister with a pin he kept in the lapel of his jacket. He did not like to prick it with a pin, because he had often heard that you should use a needle. By the time he had pricked the blister, it was dark, and he still had not come to the lonnen.

Half an hour later, he knew that he was lost. Far away below him he could see the lights of many collieries, but he could not make them out. His sense of direction began to fail him in the dark, but eventually he came to a farm, and saw a man going from byre to byre with a lantern. He did not dare to enter the farmyard, because the dogs had already begun to bark; but he called out and the man heard him. He came over and stood the lantern on the wall.

' Lad, tha gave me a fright shouting out like that! What on earth are ye up to on the fells at this time of night? '

' I want to get to Hesleyside.'

' Hesleyside—man, that's a lang way out. Which way did ye come? '

' That way.'

' Ye'll hev to turn back, hinny. And when ye come to a little turning to the left, that's Sandy Lonnen.'

' I'll be all right if I can find the lonnen.'

' Look for the signpost. Mind, it's not easy to see. Hev you got any matches? '

' No.'

' Why, here, tak' these, and strike one or two when ye come to the turning. Ye must be a plucky little beggar to be wandering about the fells by yersel' at this hour. Take care, hinny. Do ye think ye can manage? '

' Yes, thanks.'

' I'd give ye a lantern, pet, but I hevvent one to spare. Mind, dinna miss that post.'

By the time Francis had found the post it was very dark; but at last he knew the road, and he hurried on as fast as his blistered foot would let him. There was nothing now between him and the village but the open fell. But a moon had got up. It was invisible behind the clouds, but its hidden light gave a faint luminousness to the sky, and he could see the path clearly. From time to time he heard sheep cough, and peewits, disturbed by the sound of his feet, got up, climbed uncertainly above him, called and fell with a hurt diving motion until they almost touched the ground. But these noises did not disturb him. He was used to them and liked them.

But as he came to the last rise before reaching the village, he heard an unexpected noise that made him halt. It was the noise of men's voices, not loud, but carrying clearly in the still darkness. As the sounds came to him he got down behind a stone wall, and began to creep forwards; and as he drew closer he heard the mingled sounds of heavy metal wheels being hauled over a stony track, of men straining and heaving, of directions and instructions being given.

'Get behind it, Toast. We'll manage better if we get behind.'

'Keep the spokes turning, Billy.'

'Put a chock in if she starts to run back.'

'Keep her moving, Toast. We're just about there.'

He seemed to recognize most of the voices—and of one of them he was sure. It was the voice of his father, and at the sound of it he did not know whether to be relieved or alarmed. Getting as close as he dared he looked over the wall and saw a huddle of dark forms bent almost double as they urged something huge and unyielding across the moor. The moor was as black as ink, but as the men moved they came to the top of the ridge and Francis saw them vaguely outlined against the pale grey sky. Then he knew what they were doing. They were hauling the gun to the edge of the great quarry that had been hollowed out years ago in the big field. He saw them struggling like soldiers over some mountain pass, manoeuvring the clumsy engine until they had got it to the lip of the quarry. There they paused, and then with a last push they toppled it over the quarry cliff. Francis heard it strike against a ledge as it fell, then it hit the water with a splash that made an old sheep that was lying near him get up and scurry away, and send up a flock of peewits, twisting and calling. Francis heard some of the men descending the quarry to make sure that the gun had sunk out of sight in the deep black pool that filled the hollow of the quarry; but he did not wait to hear or see any more.

Forgetting his blister he dashed across the gateway that the men had left open on their way to the quarry, and ran home.

Although the door was open and the light on, he thought at first that there was no one in, but as he closed the door he heard his mother call from the pantry: 'Is that you, Simon?'

' No, it's me—Francis.'

' What ? '

She came out of the pantry with the kettle in her hand.

' What on earth are you doing here ? Who's brought you back ? "

' Nobody. I've walked home.'

' What on earth for ? '

' I didn't like it at my uncle's.'

' And you've walked home—by yourself ? '

' Yes.'

' And what about your aunt ? Does she know what you've done ? '

' No.'

' Well, of all the daft tricks ! Where's your things ? '

' I left them.'

' Now we're in a pickle ! I bet they're searching high and low for you. Your da will go sky-high when he comes in. Here, get this into you, and for heaven's sake get into bed. My, there'll be ructions about this. Don't let him clap eyes on you, or else you'll cop it. You've done a few daft things, but this beats the band.'

He went dumbly off to bed, and lay awake waiting for his father to come in. All his dreams of a kind welcome fell away from him, and he began to see his escapade in its true light, as something not daring and brave but unbelievably stupid. He knew that his father would not beat him—he had never been beaten in his life—but he was ashamed to have acted foolishly. He lay awake waiting to hear himself reproved and censured for a silly, homesick and feckless baby.

Presently his father came in.

' What do you think, Simon ? ' he heard his mother say. ' Here's our Francis walked all the way by himself from his aunt Zillah's . . . Aye, and he never told them he was off. They'll be turning the place upside-down to find him. Somebody will have to go to the police-station, and get them to telephone through.'

'The police-station! Dot, that's the last place I want to go to, tonight of all nights. What made him come back?'

'I think he was homesick.'

'Now we're in a bit of a stumour. Dot, I daren't show my face in the police-station, not after what we've been up to.'

'Somebody will have to go.'

Francis lay wondering what would happen next, but to his relief he heard his mother say, 'I'll slip over to our Elizabeth's and see if Jacob will gan for us. You get off to bed just in case anybody starts asking questions.'

But his father stayed up till she came back. 'Jacob was full of excuses as you might expect, but David's gone. By, I wish our Francis had as much sense as David. He gives me mair trouble than tongue can tell.'

'He's put us in a pickle this time,' said his father. 'Many a one would give him a good hiding for this. Still, fair's fair, Dot, he's not the only one that's taken the law in his own hands today. If the coppers knew what we've been up to, I'd be the one to get the walloping, not him. Let him sleep. He'll be tired—and after all it's not every lad of his age that can do a ten-mile walk in the dark.'

17

The Interview

HAPPILY the strike did not last very long. Mr. Kirtley did not like the new agreement the men had made with the owners.

' This business isn't finished yet, Dot,' he said. ' There'll be a lot of trouble in the coal industry yet. I can see it coming as plain as daylight.'

But most of the men were only too pleased to get back to work. Hesleyside gained a new lease of life, and no sooner had the pit opened again than Francis had a letter from the Director of Education telling him that he had got through the second examination and had to go to the Johnston School in Durham for an interview.

The interview was held on the last day of the holidays. Francis's mother said he could go by bus if he liked. A man from the Broom had bought two buses and was running a regular service between Hesleyside and Durham. But it was a fine day, and Francis said he would like to walk.

It was the kind of day he loved to be out in, bright and clear and windy. He crossed the railway lines that went up the drift on the fells, went round the edge of the Bleezer and through the Broom. It was funny but ever since the buses had started to run there had been less fighting between the Side and the Broom. There had not been one good fight since the day Cutty Bilton and his gang tried to take the heap. Although there were boys playing in the street none took any notice of him.

Once he was out of the Broom he took the road that followed the Deerness. He liked the name Deerness. It had a sweet sound to him, but the river itself was dirty. One hot day he had tried to swim there and had come out of the water with specks of oil sticking to him. After Neville's Cross he began the long descent down the Peth. It was not as dark now as it used to be. They were cutting down the trees to widen the road for the buses.

The Grammar School was half-way up a steep cobbled street that climbed the riverside opposite the Cathedral and as he went he looked up at the tall, gloomy houses that lined it. The day had grown warmer, and women were sitting at the open upper windows. One of them was nursing a baby and eating an apple. As he went by, conscious of his best clothes and the strangeness of the place, she contemptuously threw down the core so that it fell in front of him. He was pleased when he had passed the women, but a new disappointment awaited him. The big door of the school was locked, and he had to go down a dark gloomy passage to get in. It was steep and narrow, more like the entrance to a gaol than a school, but once he had passed through it he found himself in a wide clean playground. Beyond it there was a shrubbery, then the river, and across the river the walls and towers of the Cathedral. He looked up at the sheer walls of the castle and the Cathedral and saw the jackdaws swirling around the towers, and he suddenly felt that this was where he wanted to be. He wanted to be in this old school with its strange entrances and its shrubbery, to be near to the Cathedral and to hear the jackdaws calling as they circled restlessly around the towers. When he had found his way inside the school and was waiting to be called for the interview, he did not feel afraid any more.

There were two masters in the room where he was interviewed. The Headmaster sat behind a big desk. He had a pencil in one hand and on the other he wore a ring, and when he rolled the pencil up and down in his palms it clacked against the ring. The other master had a white bald head and a white face, with big lips and a shrewd and calculating look.

Francis wondered if the Headmaster would ask about the examination papers he had spoilt, but instead he questioned him about his father and the books he had read. Then suddenly he said, ' I understand that you have done some French in your school. Is that so?'

'Yes, sir.'

'Well, that's unusual. We don't get many boys of your age who have done any French. Can you read French—can you pronounce it?'

'I think I can, sir.'

'Then you'd better try him out, Mr. Cohen, and see what he can do. Have you got something reasonably easy there for him?'

'Start reading at the top of the page,' Mr. Cohen said brusquely.

'Page twenty-one, sir?'

'Of course, of course.'

Francis began reading. The first sentences were easy.

'*Jean est un soldat. Il est un soldat dans la guerre. Il porte un fusil. Il a été blessé dans la guerre. Il a une . . .*'

He stopped. The next word puzzled him, and running his eye along the line he saw a second word he could not recognize. He managed to pronounce the first hard word—

'*Il a une blessure . . .*' but the second word filled him with confusion.

'What do you think *blessure* means?' asked Mr. Cohen.

'I think it might mean a wound, sir.'

'Very good. Very good indeed. Go on.'

But he could not. The next word was *poitrine*. He had never seen it before. It had no connexion with any other French word he had met. He stopped dead, and felt all his confidence going out of him.

'Read on.'

'I can't, sir,' he said, blushing at his failure.

But Mr. Cohen took the book from him and smiled. 'Don't worry,' he said. 'It's a hard word for a little fellow like you. Anybody would forgive you for not knowing that word.'

'What does it mean, sir?'

'The chest. *Poitrine*—the chest. That's how to pronounce it. Never mind. You've done very well.'

'Finished, Mr. Cohen?' asked the Headmaster.

'Yes, sir. I'm satisfied.'

'Good, then off you go, my boy. And close the door after you.'

He began to rub his hands together again and Francis could hear the pencil clacking against the ring. He said good-bye politely and went out of the room with his heart swelling. He had not disgraced himself after all. Mr. Cohen had admitted it was a hard word. He wished he had known so that he could have seemed brilliant . . . but he had not made a fool of himself. When he came out into the playground he lifted his eyes to the Cathedral, and as if to celebrate the end of the interview, the bells began to sound. They were doing no more than ringing the hour, but to Francis it sounded like an acclamation.

He set out to walk home, avoiding the road, and taking the paths across the fields. He knew these paths that went in and out of the little streets that straggled on the edge of the city, skirted allotments and little workshops, then went under bridges and by ditches until they came out into the open country above the city. The day was clear and sweet, with a soft wind blowing in from the fells. He could scarcely feel the movement of the air until he was clear of the houses, but then he felt it moving above and around him, driving little clouds like boats before it, and flowing round him like a warm tide. It seemed to pour in a gentle but strong flood, above him, past him, and in a strange way into him, as if it entered him and filled him with vigour.

It was as if the year and the land were waking and stirring, and his own life was changing with them, as if he had somehow passed a frontier and a boundary, almost a crisis. He had never felt that he was destined to live the life that his father had lived, or his father's friends, or even David, dear though his cousin was to him. Now he was more certain than ever that a different kind of future was awaiting him, a life not bounded by the pit and all that the pit meant, but opening and widening with new hopes and aspirations, a world of knowledge and learning and creating. As he walked he felt that the clear sky, the vastness of the valley before him, and the greater vastness of the enormous fells, even the living presence of the vivid green shoots of the new grass beneath his feet, were all tokens of his new found liberty, images of something unfolding and growing, alive with endless possibilities of new happiness and new conquests. He was neither tired nor hungry, but filled with an elation that stayed with him even when he was climbing the cindery path over the Bleezer, and had entered the labyrinth of the colliery streets.

18

The New Policeman

NEARLY everybody in Hesleyside had some idea who had moved the gun, although few knew exactly where it had been hidden; and everyone enjoyed the joke, except the Councillors who were furious at being made to look so foolish. They tried hard to find out what had happened to it, but the secret was well kept. In the end they gave up the search, and took it out of Mr. Cotterell, the Hesleyside policeman, and blamed him for not keeping a better eye on their property. Someone must have taken notice of their complaint, because a few weeks later he was moved to another part of the county, and a new constable took his place. The new bobby made it his business to keep a sharp look-out for all possible offenders, and it was Francis's bad luck to be one of the first to fall foul of him.

One of the jobs that he still hated was going shopping for his mother to the Broom. It was a dull errand and he would do everything he could to make the journey less boring. He tried to vary his route, and instead of keeping to the main road, he took to squeezing through the fence of broken sleepers that divided the railway from the road and crossing the lines instead of going under the bridge. He liked being on top of the embankment, and running across the lines when a train was coming.

One day, seeing a train coming, he put a halfpenny on the rails and lay down on the embankment until it passed. He had done this before, hoping the halfpenny would be squashed to the size of a penny and be big enough to put in a slot-machine, but the miracle had never happened. Nor did it this time. When the train had passed he saw that all he had done was to ruin a good halfpenny. He put it in his pocket and was squeezing through the railings to get back on to the road when he saw a policeman watching him.

The sight of a policeman at close quarters was enough to put fear into any Hesleyside boy. Francis was doubly alarmed. He had been caught trespassing, and caught by a policeman whom he could not recognize.

'Come here! Come here!' said the bobby. 'What do you think you're doing?'

'I'm going to the Broom.'

'And is that the way you always take?'

'No.'

'I should hope not. Do you know what trespassing is? Eh? Do you know you're supposed to keep off the railway? What's your name?'

'Francis Kirtley.'

He thought for a moment of giving a false name. He had often heard boys say that you could get away without a summons if you gave a wrong name, but the words came out without thinking.

'Francis Kirtley, eh? And where do you live? In Hesleyside?'

'Yes, sir.'

'Can you read?'

'Yes, sir.'

'Can you read what that notice says? Go on. Look at it.'

There was hardly any need for Francis to turn his head. He had looked at the notice so many times that he knew it by heart.

L.N.E.R.
No unauthorized persons allowed on this line.
By Order.

He recited it for the policeman.

'Good. Now give me your full name and address.'

To Francis's horror he took out his notebook and entered the details there.

'You'll hear more about this, young feller,' he said. 'Now

go on, get away as sharp as you can, or else I'll give you a good wallop. I've heard about you Hesleyside lads. You think you can do just what you want. But not with me! You've picked on the wrong feller this time. Now go on and beat it!'

Francis did not dare to mention the incident to his father, but, by coincidence the name of the new policeman came up the same night. It was P.C. Howie, and he was the man who had taken the place of the disgraced Mr. Cotterell. He had already made himself greatly disliked. For years some of the men had been in the habit of gathering on free afternoons in the fields beyond the Bleezer and running a gambling school. Francis had often seen them standing in a circle and tossing pennies in the air. Old Mr. Cotterell had turned a blind eye to the sport, but P.C. Howie was determined to break up the school. He had taken to spying on them, and when he had taken the names of all the men he could identify, he would come out of hiding and tell them that he was giving them a summons. All the men hated him for it, and thought it was a sneaking way of going on.

To Francis it was one more proof that the new bobby meant business. He felt more sure than ever that he would get his summons, and hardly dared to go home from school in case the fatal letter had arrived.

Fortunately no summons came, but Mr. Kirtley knew nothing of that affair. He continued to hold his bad opinion of the new policeman, and he had many an argument with Grandpa Hewitt about him. They had got over their difference about Armistice Day, but they rarely saw eye to eye.

'Why shouldn't he break up the gambling school?' asked the old man. 'Why shouldn't he? You tell me that. He's just doing his job and the more credit to him.'

'It's a pity he couldn't find something better to do with his time. What harm is there in a bit of innocent gambling?'

'Gambling's never innocent.'

'It's come to a pretty pass if a feller canna enjoy hissel after slaving away in the pit.'

'Gambling's gambling. It's sinful in the eyes of the Lord.'

Gambling and drinking were the two things that put him in a passion.

'Hout, the man's nowt but a nosey parker!'

'It's his job. If it was a man in the pit that wasn't doing his job you'd have enough to say.'

'I know the kind he is, Grandpa. It's not the rights and the wrongs that he's worried about. Promotion—that's what he's after. The mair poor fellers he can fetch up the sooner he'll get his stripes. I tell you—he'll get a sneck afore his snout if he carries on like this.'

'Aye, ye were always a lawless lot.'

'Nowt the sort. We always lived peaceably enough afore he started poking his nose in. He's asking for trouble, this joker.'

'You'll be the ones that'll get into trouble. You've taken the law into your hands afore this.'

'What do you mean, Grandpa?'

'Never you mind. Never you mind.'

'Is it that gun you're thinking about?'

'Yes, that among other things.'

'It'll tak' a better man than him to get to the bottom of that.'

'That's what you think. You haven't heard the last of that business yet.'

'For heaven's sake, stop bickering you two. I don't know what it is, but I canna put the pair of you in the same room without an argument.'

Mrs. Kirtley was more successful than on the previous occasion in reconciling or at least silencing her father and her husband. But Francis was worried. He knew that it was not often his grandfather was proved in the wrong.

19

Mr. Kirtley Gets a New Marra

THE strike had one unexpected consequence for Mr. Kirtley. It left him without a working partner. All the men in Hesleyside worked with a partner, a ' marra ' as he was called, and for years Francis's father had been paired with Mr. Ainslie, one of the original Jolly Boys; but before the strike had come to an end Mr. Ainslie had decided that he did not want to work any longer in the mine. His brother had found him a job in Coventry and he had taken it.

100

It was David's father, of all people, who found Mr. Kirtley a new marra. He did not come to Russell Street often, although he lived only across the street. Mrs. Kirtley had never liked him, and never ceased to wonder what it was that had made her sister marry him; but it was not the cold welcome that put Jacob off. He was far too insensitive to know what anyone thought of him. It was rather because he and his brother-in-law had little in common.

Francis was drawing a map on the kitchen table when his uncle came in. He loved drawing and tracing maps, following with his pencil the fascinating undulations of the coastline, letting it sink into the hollows of the bays and sweep out over the promontories, and indicating the sea with a blue fringe. His uncle came over and looked condescendingly at his work.

' And what's our Francis up to now, eh? ' he said.

Francis winced. His uncle's silly way of speaking seemed to imply that he was doing something that he did not want to be caught at.

' Books, books! This lad of yours, Dot, he always hes his nose in a book. That'll get tha nowhere. That'll not stand tha in much stead when tha gets into the pit. It would be mair menseful to be getting a bit of exercise. Putting a bit of muscle on them limmers, eh? '

' I like drawing maps, Uncle Jacob.'

' Pooh! Tha winna find any maps to draw once tha gets off to work.'

' Leave him alone, Jacob,' said Mrs. Kirtley. ' If it gives him pleasure let him enjoy it.'

' Aye, enjoy thisel while tha can. When tha hes as much on thy plate as thy uncle tha'll hev plenty to worry about.'

' Rubbish,' said Mrs. Kirtley. She could not stand her brother-in-law and his silly ways. ' You have nothing to worry about.'

' Aye, if he's as good a pitman as his uncle he'll be a good 'un.'

' For God's sake, stop bragging, Jacob. Anybody would think you were the only feller in Hesleyside that did a day's work.'

But as usual Jacob was not listening.

' Where's Simon, then ? '

' He's at the Club.'

' You wouldn't catch me wasting my time there. Not me. I can keep in good fettle without that muck. Is he still looking for a marra ? '

' Yes.'

' Why, I've just popped in to say that Michael Blamires is looking for somebody to work with. They should make a good pair.'

Francis looked up angrily. Why was it that everything his uncle said sounded like either a boast or an insult ? But he suddenly remembered where he had heard the name Blamires before. That was the man that his grandfather had recognized in the darkness. Francis remembered his words—' a man your father should take a few lessons from '. He forgot his annoyance at his uncle and waited to hear more.

But his mother said quickly, ' I'll tell him,' and then changed the subject. She did not like to be beholden to her brother-in-law. ' How's our Elizabeth these days ? ' she went on.

' There's nowt wrang with her. I nivver worry myself about her. She can tak' care of hersel. Why, I've done my good turn for the day. I'll be off.'

' It's a good job she can look after herself,' said Mrs. Kirtley as soon as he had gone. ' Her husband winna look after her. I've never seen anybody more taken up with number one than him. I'm ashamed of him, even though he is my brother-in-law. I think he's the most sackless feller that ever I saw in all my born days. What our Elizabeth saw in him, I'll never understand, not if I live to be a hundred.'

Mr. Blamires became Mr. Kirtley's marra, but he was unlike any other marra that Francis had ever known. Once the men had begun to work together he would come to Russell Street every Friday night to collect his share of the pay, and the two men would sit talking about their work, what kind of ' cavil ' or working place they had, the behaviour of the deputies who super-

MR. KIRTLEY GETS A NEW MARRA

vised them, and the putters who worked for them; and sometimes when they had had a good week and were feeling in a mood
to celebrate, Mr. Kirtley would say, 'Come on, Michael, let's
have a bit of Robbie Burns afore we gan to bed. Give us a few
lines.'

Then a strange change came over Mr. Blamires. He would sit
back in his chair and close his eyes and begin to recite. When
he was talking about the pit he used the language of the miners,
but when he spoke his poems, he did it in a voice that had no
trace of 'pitmatic' in it, a voice that he had learnt to use somewhere else. It was a Scottish voice, very musical and clear. He
could go through the whole of 'Tam O'Shanter', and 'The
Cotter's Saturday Night', but what Mr. Kirtley liked best of all
to hear was 'A Man's a Man for a' That'.

'Come on, Michael,' he would say, 'give us "A Man's a
Man". That's the stuff I like to hear. If I had my way, Michael,
I'd make every colliery manager—aye and every coal owner in
the land—listen to that, and take it in.'

Francis had never known anyone with a memory like this.
No matter what poem Mr. Blamires began, he would finish it,
and he would go from beginning to end without hesitating or
stumbling. His memory was perfect.

That such a man, with gifts like these, should be content to
work in the pit was a mystery to Francis, but he soon found that
there were other mysteries surrounding Mr. Blamires. One day
his father asked him to take a message to his new marra, and he
saw the Blamires' house for the first time.

When he went in he could see only one corner of the room.
Inside the door someone had built a wide wooden screen that
ran from floor to ceiling—the colliery people called them
'bradishes' and put them up to keep out draughts. This was the
biggest Francis had ever seen. He heard Mr. Blamires telling him
to come in, and when he had turned the screen he saw why it was
so big. Behind it was a bed, and in the bed, almost filling it, was
a woman with a broad face and bulky shoulders and twisted,
sinewy hands. Her large body was heaped over with bedclothes

and a big quilt made of squares of coloured wools, and over the quilt were spread sheets and sheets of newspapers. The room was hot. There was an enormous fire blazing in the grate. The room smelt of the suffocating heat, and of the ointments and salves that

stood on a little table by the side of the bed. Newspaper had been pinned around the light to keep the glare from falling on the woman's face, but even in the shaded light Francis could see the wallpaper by the bedside scrawled over with notes and calculations, the names of horses, lists of figures, sums to be added.

Francis looked round the room in bewilderment. The heat, the suffocating closeness, the smell of the unfamiliar medicines, the sight of the huge woman under the piled mound of bedclothes, confused him, and he stood stock still at the edge of the bradish.

' And who's this, then ? ' asked the woman, lowering her newspaper and looking over her spectacles. He had expected her to speak with the exhausted whisper of an invalid, but her voice was loud and bold.

' It's Simon's lad. My new marra's young lad, Francis.'

' Francis, eh ? That's a lah-di-dah name now, isn't it ? What's your da fancying for the big race then ? '

' I don't suppose he knows that, Bella,' said Mr. Blamires. He was sitting by the fire as if he was its guardian, and was there to keep it well supplied with coal. He spoke very softly and gently to his wife.

' Why shouldn't he ? Your da likes a bet now and then, doesn't he ? '

' He sometimes puts something on the coupons, Mrs. Blamires.'

' Coupons ? Football coupons ? Pooh, he'll never make anything out of them. Doesn't he like to put a bob now and then on the gee-gees ? '

' I think he does.'

' I should think he does. Here, reach me that bit of paper.'

He handed it to her. Her hands were twisted and stiff but she could still write with them. She wrote something on the paper and gave it to him.

' Tell your da to back that one for the big race next week if he wants to rake in a bit. Can you read ? '

' Yes, Mrs. Blamires.'

' He's a good reader, Bella. He's a good little scholar, is Francis.'

' Is he now ? Well, good luck to him. Keep it up, bonny lad. Here, put a bit more coal on that fire, Michael. I canna abide a poor fire.'

She turned back to her paper, and Francis delivered his message. But he could not help looking towards the bed as he spoke. He wondered how the woman could endure the heat under that enormous mound of bedclothes. Did Mr. Blamires sleep there ?

The bed was so filled with the vast body of his wife that it was hard to see how anyone else could get in. And the smells of the medicines and salves were still strong and troubled him. He was glad when he escaped into the fresh air.

'Did you give Mr. Blamires the message?' asked Mr. Kirtley when he reached home.

'Yes, and I brought one back for you.'

'From Michael?'

'No, from Mrs. Blamires.'

'It'll be a tip, I'll bet a dollar. What did she say?'

'She said I had to give you this.'

'Aye,' said Mr. Kirtley, opening the note. 'Just what I thought. It's a tip for the big race. She was in bed, was she?'

'Yes, she was reading the papers.'

'Studying the form, I expect. She's a wonder is Bella. She's been bedfast for years, but she knows more about horse-racing than any of the men.'

'Does she bet?'

'I should think she does. She's the bookies' best friend is Bella . . . But ye canna blame the poor woman. Michael says it's the only thing that keeps her alive.'

'Does he bet as well?'

'Nivver. It's bad enough with one in the house. If he started as well, they'd both be in the workhouse in double-quick time. He hasn't much of a life has Michael, but he nivver grumbles. He's got a heart of gold, that lad.'

'He's got a strange name, hasn't he, da?'

'A strange name for a strange feller.'

'How is he strange?'

'He's a mystery man, is Michael. He's a puzzle-the-world.'

'In what way?'

'Man-alive, ivverything about him's a mystery. He doesn't even know what his own mother and father were.'

'Has he never seen them?'

'No, he has no more idea who they were than the man in the moon. And he never will now.'

Being a mystery man did not stop Mr. Blamires from being a good marra, and Mr. Kirtley and he got on well together. Francis, too, was fond of him, and he took to spending more and more time with him. Mr. Blamires never went out to the Club, for he did not like to leave his wife alone for too long. Most of his free time he spent indoors and he was glad of the boy's company. They often played cards or checkers together—checkers more often than cards for Mr. Blamires was a good player, very clever at thinking out ingenious moves, and Francis enjoyed pitting his wits against him. At first he disliked the way Mrs. Blamires would interrupt their games, asking for a new pencil, a missing page in the *Northern Echo*, a sheet of paper she had mislaid or some medicine she could not lay her hands on; but Mr. Blamires was never put out by her interruptions, and Francis

began to fall in with his patient ways, even jumping up in the middle of a game to help her. At first he had been disconcerted by her abrupt manner, but he found that she was not often petulant. More often she was jolly. Being bedfast seemed to have made her not ill-tempered and cantankerous, but serene, fond of good-natured gossip, and absorbed with the business of picking winners. Francis began to feel that she liked having him in the house, and was as fond of his company as her husband was. She liked to know how the games were going, and what he was doing at school; and when her husband read or recited, although she seemed to be taking no notice, and went on reading her newspapers and scribbling on the wallpaper, he knew that she was listening and in her own way taking as much pleasure in the readings as he was.

20

A Day on the Fells

THE days between Easter and Whitsuntide were warm and dry, and the streets were forsaken as the boys took to the fields, thrusting their hands into every holly and hawthorn bush, marking where the larks came down and quartering the rough pastures till they found the little brown eggs hidden beneath the bent grasses. They ventured along the dry 'lonnens' and into the forbidden woods, trying to find where the pheasants had laid, fearful of the silence, and expecting always to see the dreaded figure of the gamekeeper rise from the undergrowth and challenge them or shoot at them with his long gun. It was said that he shot needles out of it that sank deep into the flesh of trespassers; but the fear of neither wound nor summons could keep them from the fields and the woods. The excitement of the Spring entered into them—the call of plover and curlew, the pungent odour of the undergrowth, the vigour of the wind blowing over the green land.

Francis could hardly bear to be indoors. He was restless and filled with a desire to be in motion, drawn to the freedom of the woods and the great fells beyond. Mr. Blamires had begun to talk to him of his youthful wanderings, and he felt an irresistible urge to see for himself the mysteries of the moors and hills.

It was this that made him fall in with a daring plan to go exploring on the fells that he had glimpsed on his lonely walk home from Satley earlier in the year. It was Nocky who put the idea into his head.

Most of the Hesleyside men worked in the main seams, and went down by cage, but a number of them were taken every day up to a big drift on the top of the fell beyond the village.

The company that owned the colliery had bought, long ago, a broken-down L.N.E.R. coach, an old-fashioned affair with missing doors and broken windows, and the men were taken in this carriage, hauled by the 'tankie', up to the drift. For some reason or other the driver always brought the coach down empty after the men had been taken to work, and it stood in a siding at the bottom of the colliery until it was time to bring them back.

Nocky's plan was to stow away in the coach when it went up empty, get clear of it before they came to the drift and then strike off across the fells. It was Saturday, the shift ended at midday, and he knew that the tankie would set off for the drift just after eleven.

The boys hid at the back of the coach until they saw the tankie backing into the siding. Crouching so that they could look along the underside of the carriage, they saw the driver fix the coupling and climb onto the footplate of the engine. When they saw his legs go out of sight, they knew it was safe to climb aboard. They hoisted themselves into the last compartment of the coach. It was easy to get in because there were no doors to it. Then they lay down flat on the dirty wooden seats, and waited for the train to move off. The driver gave a short blast on the

whistle, and the coach began to move slowly off on the steep
climb to the drift, past the allotments, past the school wall, and
then out into the open country.

The boys lay stretched out on the seats, hardly daring at first
to look up, then lifting their heads to watch their progress. The
climb was steep and winding, through little copses, past the first
level crossing where the road to Ushaw sloped away, then
through shallow cuttings dotted with coltsfoot and a few prim-
roses. For a while they dared to sit up, but at last the train began
to slow as it drew near to the drift. Francis knew it was easier
to climb onto the train without being noticed than to get off it;
but Nocky knew what to do. He knew that when they came to
a stop the driver would get down and go over to the offices to
wait for the men. Peering through the open door he saw the
driver get down and walk over to the little shed, wiping his hands
on a piece of oily waste. Then he gave Francis a sign. They
jumped down on the blind side, and hid in the gorse bushes.
Then from a safe distance they saw the men climb aboard and
the train begin to reverse slowly and cautiously down the incline
back to the colliery. When it was out of sight they got up and
made off across the empty fell.

They came first to a beck, and working their way upwards came upon a little pool no more than two feet in diameter and overhung with grasses, its surface curiously dimpled. The dimplings on the surface were where the water, issuing from underground, pressed upwards in a spring. Francis could see the dark sand at the bottom of the pool stirring as the water bubbled

up from it. He plunged his hand into the water, and when he put his fingers down on the sand he could feel the spring pulsing and rising past them.

'It's a spring! It's the source! Let's follow the beck as far as we can.'

They retraced their steps, following the water as it went twisting and leaping down the fell side, almost vanishing into dark gullies, narrowing between stony gorges and spilling in miniature waterfalls.

'Let's make a dam!' said Francis; and they set to work to build a little weir of heather shoots, stones and sods, until the imprisoned water could no longer be held back but spilt in a foot-high cascade over the rim of the dam. Then in a spasm of destructiveness they pulled down their work, and watched the water pour through the breach and sweep everything before it.

Following the beck as it ran down the slope they came upon something that Francis had never seen before but recognized immediately. It was an air-shaft, like the chimney in the garden that his father had explained to him. He remembered his father saying that one or two of them could be found on the fells. But unlike the shaft in the village this was in a bad state of repair. Most of the wall around it had crumbled. The gaps had been roughly blocked with branches and bushes, and across the mouth of the shaft rough boards had been laid.

They scrambled through the gaps and stood on the edge of the opening, trying to look down through the planks. Remembering his father's caution Francis kept clear of the edge, but Nocky ventured farther in, and noticed that the planks were no longer nailed down, but could be lifted clear. Lifting two or three of them he peered down into the blackness, then, seeing nothing, took a loose brick and dropped it. It disappeared soundlessly. There was no splash, no thud. It was as if it had fallen into a bottomless pit.

' It's hundreds of feet deep ! ' cried Nocky, jumping clear as if he, too, were in danger of being swallowed up by the hole. 'Come on, let's get away from it.'

They had been so absorbed in their play that they did not notice how the day had changed ; but by the time they had come to the road that Francis had taken on his way from Satley, the horizon was beginning to be engulfed by sweeping curtains of rain. A few minutes later and they were driven to shelter behind a stone wall.

The wall was a poor shelter. The fell was bare and open, and the rain was falling steeply. Within a few minutes they were wet. They had pulled their jackets up to make a kind of hood but the water soon began to seep through. There was nothing to do but to huddle closer to the wall and hope that the rain would pass.

They were sitting like this when along the road came a man with a sack over his head. Francis did not recognize him but as soon as the man spoke he realized that there was something in his speech that was familiar.

' What are you two lads doing there ? '

'Trying to keep dry.'

'What are ye doing out in this weather?'

'We've just been for a walk.'

'A walk! Why, ye've picked a canny day for a walk. Where do ye come from?'

'Hesleyside.'

'The colliery?'

'Yes.'

'Wait a bit, I think I've seen thoo afore this, haven't I?' said the man, looking at Francis. 'Are you the lad that got lost just about here one night a bit since?'

Francis knew now where he had met the man before.

'Yes.'

'I thought I recognized tha. By lad ye must be a proper little tramp—a proper Wandering Willie, eh? Fancy coming across thoo again! But ye'll both get sumpen wet if ye stop here.'

'Mebbe it'll fair up,' said Nocky.

'Not this side of tea-time. Ye'd better come with me and get dry. Lad, ye look like a couple of drowned rats.'

He took them across two fields, through a little patch of dripping woodland and then up to the doorway of a grey stone farm-house.

'What's the fire like, Beattie?' he called as he went through the door, dumping his wet sack just inside the room.

'It's a good fire,' called his wife from inside. 'What are you asking for?'

'I've just fetched a couple of young lads in out of the rain,' he answered. 'They're in a bonny bad state. Take your coats off, hinnies, and come up to the fire.'

By now his wife had come into the kitchen. 'Mercy on us,' she cried. 'What on earth are ye doing out here in this weather?'

'We were out for a walk.'

'Ye've picked a nice day for a walk, heven't ye? But we'll soon get you dry again. Heavens, ye'll both get double pneumonia if you try to get home in them wet things. Just sit here, hinnies, and I'll mek a cup of tea for ye.'

The boys sat up to the fire, and looked round. It was the first farm kitchen that Francis had ever been in, and he could not keep his eyes off the legs of bacon hanging from the ceiling. There was a very big heavy table in the middle of the room, with odd chairs grouped round it, and on the mantelpiece photographs of the farmer and his wife at their wedding, looking stiff and unnatural in their best clothes. The room was full of strange smells, of cooking and burning wood and of pig food being boiled up somewhere. The kind farmer's wife gave them tea and big slices of bread and butter.

'It's a lucky thing that I came across you lads,' said the farmer when they had finished. 'I'm just yoking the hoss to take a few things down to the village and I can give you a lift. I think I can find a couple of sacks to keep the worst of the rain off ye. Are ye fit?'

It was still raining as they jogged down to the village, but there was enough light for Francis to notice one thing. The quarry where the gun lay sunken was on one side of the track, and the ruined ventilation shaft on the other; but they were close together and not more than a quarter of a mile separated them.

21

The End of the Gun

FRANCIS expected to get into trouble for being away so long, but he returned to find his father preoccupied with more serious matters.

'I knew that feller would make trouble the minute I saw him. He's had it in for the men of this place from the word go.'

Francis knew that his father was talking about the new policeman. For a moment he feared that his summons had come, but his mother went on:

'How much do they reckon he's found out, then?'

'They say that he has a good idea where the gun is, and he's got a few names as well.'

'Has he got yours?'

'Aye and Toast's, and Matty Howden's and a few mair.'

'Where did he get them from?'

'It doesn't tak' much guessing. Once that brother-in-law of yours got to know it was sure to be all over the colliery. He's the most sackless clown that ivver walked. Nowt's a secret once he gets hold of it.'

'What's going to happen then, Simon?'

'I dinna suppose he can do anything till he's found the gun. But once they've laid hands on it, we'll be in Queer Street, Dot. They say he's going to make a search next week. Well, if we're copped, we're copped. But if only that man of your Elizabeth's had kept his mouth shut, he would never have found it.'

'But what will happen if the gun isn't found, da?' asked Francis.

'He'll be fettled. No evidence—no charge . . . But what do you know about this? This is not supposed to be for you. Don't you go talking about what you've heard, mind.'

' I won't say anything, da.'

But he knew he was lying. Already a plan was forming in his mind and he knew that he would have to speak with David about it.

He ran across the street and fortunately found his cousin alone.

' David,' he said, ' have you heard about the gun—and what the bobby is going to do ? '

' Yes, I've heard about it.'

' Did you know that my da was one of the men that took it away ? '

' Yes.'

' How did you know ? '

' I heard my father telling my mother about it.'

' Do you know where they put it ? '

' No.'

' I do.'

' How did you get to know ? '

' I saw them putting it there the night I walked home from my uncle's at Satley.'

' And you never told anybody ? '

' No.'

' I wish my da was as good at keeping a secret as you are, Francis. I'm ashamed of him. Everybody is. They say he's the one that let the cat out of the bag.'

' David, I want you to come and see where it is.'

' Now ? '

' No, tomorrow night. I want you to come, David, because I want your help.'

The next day was Sunday, and as soon as they had had dinner they went up to the quarry. Francis lay down with his head leaning out over the edge of the quarry face and got David to do the same.

' That's where it is.'

' Where, in the pond ? '

' Yes. Can you see it yet ? '

' No.'

'Keep staring. There—in the deepest part. Can you see that dark shape?'

'I can see it now. Good lord, I would never have thought of looking there.'

'But the bobby will find it. He knows it's somewhere in this pond.'

'What are you going to do, Francis?'

'I want us to get it out.'

'By ourselves? We'll never do it.'

'But a gang would.'

'If it was big enough. But what do you do when you've got it out?'

'I've found another place to hide it. Come on, I'll show you.'

They crossed the track and Francis took David through the heather and gorse until they came to the shaft that he and Nocky had found.

'That's the place, David,' he said.

'How on earth did you find this?'

' Nocky and I found it a few days back.'

' Is it big enough ? '

' I don't know. But the planks are loose, look. You can take them up. If we get the gun down there nobody will find it and the men won't have to go to prison.'

' Do you think we can get it from the quarry to here ? '

' It's downhill.'

' Let's try it, Francis. I know, Billy Fineday has some grappling-hooks. He was going to use them when they thought Nocky had thrown himself in the colliery pond last year. Ask him for them.'

' What should I say to him ? '

' I don't know. Make something up. If he won't let you have them, I'll ask. He'll let me have anything. You get the ropes, Francis, and I'll get the gang.'

' How many do you think we'll want ? '

' Twenty, at least—but we'll get them. We'll get more than twenty.'

By the end of the day the plans were completed. Nocky was one of the first to join the gang. Billy Fineday, the school-caretaker, was not at work, but Nocky broke into the boiler-house and took the grappling-hooks and the ropes. Francis and he carried them up to the quarry, keeping away from the roads and cutting across the fields. Francis lay down once more on the edge of the quarry and under his directions Nocky cast the hooks until they caught on something. They could not be sure it was the gun they had hooked, but short of going into the water themselves, this was the best they could do. Then they left the free ends of the ropes lying on the ground, but covered them with dirt and stones, hoping they would go unnoticed till the next day.

Meanwhile David had mustered his gang. Among them were Chris and Billy Ord, three or more members of the football team, boys who would do anything for David, and more than a dozen others whose fathers had good cause for disliking P.C. Howie.

The next day just after dark they all assembled on the fell. There were between twenty and thirty, all tough wiry boys with good muscles and strong shoulders. They had come up to the quarry in small groups of two and three to avoid suspicion, and now lay hidden in the gorse waiting for orders.

It was David who took charge. He uncovered the ropes and made sure that there was no likelihood of their being disturbed. Then he detailed two of the younger boys to keep a watch on the road and give warning of the approach of any stranger, and divided the rest of the gang into two groups.

'Don't get excited,' he said. 'Pull when I say and don't let it slide back once it's started to move. Now, pull!'

To their surprise, whatever it was that the hooks were fastened to began to move, but as soon as the first effort was relaxed it began to slide back.

'Hold it!' said David, going from group to group. 'Some of you hold back ready to steady it when the others have pulled. Ready? Pull!'

The gun moved again, and this time it was held. It was still deep in the water but after a few more pulls they could see the barrel beginning to show above the surface.

'We've got it,' said David. 'Dig your heels in and hold it. Pull again!'

Slowly the barrel nosed its way out of the pond. By now it had come to rest on some invisible ledge, and they all took a rest. But not for long. They were impatient to see it clear of the water. There was no need now for David to urge them on. They grunted and hauled and at last the gun was clear of the water and free.

At that moment one of the boys who was keeping watch came softly over the damp earth and told David that someone was coming along the road.

'Get down, everybody,' he whispered. 'Keep hold of the ropes but get down.'

They all flattened themselves on the cold ground. In the silence Francis could hear the water dripping from the barrel of the gun on to the ground—pit, pit, pit—like the beating of his heart, and the sound of the stranger's footsteps going evenly and regularly along the sandy track. They went on evenly, pace by pace, then grew fainter and fainter. Whoever it was that was walking along the road had seen and suspected nothing. They all lay still till the sound had died away. Then they hauled the gun out of the quarry and down towards the airshaft.

It was now Nocky's turn to take over.

He had one of the ropes tied round his waist, and in the darkness crawled to the far side of the mouth of the shaft. One by one he pulled the loose boards clear, and passed them back. When all the planks had been removed the boys got behind the gun and began to heave it through the gap in the shaft wall. Nocky had now undone the rope round his waist and David saw to it that the gun was unhooked. They tipped it forward, heaved and felt it toppling, and as soon as it began to drop they all fell back. It hesitated for a second, then heeled over, and fell. They heard it hurtling down in the darkness, hitting the sides of the shaft, dislodging loose stones, and then it vanished almost as soundlessly as the stone that Nocky had thrown the other day. When they were sure it had disappeared, Nocky put back the planks, and the boys began to scuffle up the loose earth around the mouth of the pit. Awed by the darkness and fearful depth of the pit into which they had pitched the gun, and incredulous of their success, the boys broke up, and in two's and three's made their way back to the colliery.

A few days later Mr. Kirtley was having his bath in front of the fire when Mr. Ord came in. He was smiling and more excited than Francis had ever seen him.

' Have ye heard what's happened, Simon ? '

' I've just come in from work. What's up ? Have the bobbies found it ? '

' Found it ? Why, man, it wasn't there ! '

' Not there ? That's impossible.'

' Impossible or not, that's the truth. They've been looking for it all day. Six of them. They fetched a sergeant and five others from Durham to drag the pond. And they've fetched nowt up but a rusty bicycle. They say the sergeant is in a flaming temper. P.C. Coppernob has made a proper flat of hissel this time.'

' Why how do ye account for it, Toast ? '

' I'm as beaten as they are. Lad, I nivver believed in good angels afore but somebody's been on the side of the Jolly Boys this time.'

' But who could have shifted it ? '

' I have no more idea than the bairn unborn. But whoever did it did us a good turn, that's a fact. Bless my soul, here we've been worrying ourselves to death about a summons, and the bird has flown! I'd give anything to know who it was that did us that good turn.'

' Well, don't ask too many questions, Toast. Let's just keep quiet and hope that the whole thing's finished and done with.'

Francis sat with his head down, pretending to read his book. He did not dare to look up in case they would read his secret in his face. He kept his eyes on his book, fearing that the men might begin to ask him questions ; but they did not speak to him, and when Mr. Ord went out he went to see David and tell him what had happened.

A few days later the triumph was complete. P.C. Howie went the way of his predecessor. He would never trouble the people of Hesleyside any more. He, too, had been transferred to another part of the county.

22

David Wins His Cap

Just before Whitsuntide David had his fourteenth birthday. The very next day he left school, and they heard that his father had put his name down for the pit.

Grandfather Hewitt was furious.

'What's this I hear, Wilson, about sending David down the pit?'

He often called Mr. Kirtley by his christian name because although he quarrelled constantly with him he had some respect for him. But he would never call Jacob by anything but his surname.

'I'm not ashamed of what I've done. I've been a pitman all my life and I've nivver been ashamed to be one. What's good enough for me is good enough for him.'

'Hasn't your wife told you that she doesn't want him in the pit?'

'It's none of her business. She's got nothing to do with it.'

'Wilson, you're a fool. You've always been one. You were born a fool, and you'll die one.'

'I know what I'm doing. I don't want anybody to tell me what to do with my family.'

'Haven't you got the sense to look round for something better for the lad? Hout, if God Himself was to try to give you advice He'd be wasting His time. You haven't a brain in your head and never will!'

'You can say what you like. I'm well liked.'

'Liked! Everybody knows you to be the most sackless feller in the colliery. I haven't any patience with you!'

But not even these insults could touch Jacob. ' Aye, aye,' he went on. ' Ye can say what you like but I'm well thought on. I've still got plenty that think the world of me.'

Realizing that no accusation, however blunt, would make him see the stupidity of his ways, the old man picked up his stick and left the house. He walked home jabbing his stick angrily into the road as if every jab was a reproof to his incorrigible son-in-law.

Unexpectedly Francis found his father siding with Jacob.

' It's all very well for folks to say " Look around and find something better ", but it's not as easy as all that. David's a clever lad, but he's not a scholar, you know, like our Francis here.'

'But he won't stop in the pit for always, will he, da ? '

' I'll be surprised if he's there for more than a couple of years. He'll keep on playing football, and somebody will pick him up. He'll be playing for Newcastle or Sunderland afore he's much older. And if he doesn't play for England in the finish I'm a Dutchman.'

' Well I hope nothing happens to him because if it does our Elizabeth will never get over it,' said his wife.

' Them's things you haven't to think about, Dot. He's lucky to be taken on, because, by sangs, things are bad nowadays, and it isn't easy to find a job.'

So David went to work, but before he did so, his mother gave him a last treat. She took him to Durham to have his photograph taken. He was photographed in his school shirt, the green-and-white colours in which he had captained the school side in the final at the Hollow Drift, but with his county cap, purple with silver piping and a tassel of silver cords. His mother liked the photograph so much that she sent it back to be tinted, and stood it, not on the mantelpiece but on the what-not in the sitting-room. And there David posed, resplendent in the colours of school and county, his arms earnestly folded on his chest, and his right foot resting on a football.

' I don't know what all the fuss and bother is about,' said his father ungenerously. ' Bless my soul, you would think he was the only lad in the world ivver to have won a medal.' But Mr.

Kirtley bought a copy of the photograph, and he was not the only one. There were many houses that sported one. Although David was now just a common pit-lad, he was still the greatest footballer Hesleyside had ever produced and they were proud of him.

23

The Mystery of Mr. Blamires

LITTLE by little Francis learnt the strange story of Mr. Blamires.

'How does he remember all those poems, da? Where does he get his memory from? You haven't a memory like that, have you?'

'I can tell you the winner of all the big races for the last few years, but I cannot recite like him. But his father wasn't a pit-man like us. No, he was an actor. He used to go about reaming off stuff just like Michael does. That's where he gets his memory. It's in the family.'

By and by Mr. Blamires himself began to fill in some of the missing details. As Mrs. Blamires lay looking through her news-papers, rubbing out names that she had pencilled on the wallpaper and entering others, her husband told Francis how his father and mother had both been on the stage, how he had always been a hindrance to them and in the end had been abandoned by them to make a living for himself as best he could. For years he had wandered like a gypsy in the wild country between England and Scotland, finding no settled work, until, as a young man, he had come to Hesleyside and become a pitman.

'Aye, and he's a good pitman,' Mr. Kirtley would say. 'He's a good marra. But he's a cut above most of us, Francis. He could have been a gentleman if he'd had the chance.'

'He still is one, if you ask me,' said Mrs. Kirtley. 'It's bred in him, ye can see that.'

There were more discoveries to be made about Mr. Blamires. Francis was fond of writing, and just as fond of making neat water-colour illustrations of the stories and articles he wrote. One day a chance remark by one of the teachers gave him the

126

idea of writing a book of his own. It was hardly a book, more like a magazine, and he called it *Looking Back—A Magazine of Historical Fun*. He wrote the whole of the magazine himself. There was an article called ' I Lived Then—The Story of Hugo the Squire ', and another called ' How to Put On a Suit of Armour '. There was a page of jokes he had picked up from other magazines under the heading ' Joker the Jester ', and an account of the building of a Norman castle under the title ' Will the Norman Explains '; and lastly one of his favourite puzzles, a series of dots numbered 1–50 which when connected made a portrait of Harold being shot in the eye by the fatal arrow.

He loved working at his book, especially in the evenings when he could spread out his pages and box of colours on the kitchen table. His father did not go out so often now in the evenings, and sometimes spent his time cobbling the family shoes. His mother was often busy cutting up old clothes to make clippings for rugs. Francis lost himself very easily in the past. Will the Norman and Joker the Jester were almost more real to him than the men who went backwards and forwards to work.

He went on copying his articles, adding impressive editorial comments.

> ' If you have a historical question you would like answered, send it to the Editor of *Looking Back*—Address: 15 Russell Street, Hesleyside Colliery, Co. Durham.'

or—

> ' Answers to the puzzles and quizzes will be found at the foot of the back page.'

He put in many hours of careful work, and was a little disappointed at the half-hearted way his mother and father received his magazine.

' Aye, it's very nice, hinny,' said his father, turning over the pages rapidly. ' You've made a tidy job of it. There's some nice

little drawings here.' But he handed it back without reading it. His mother gave him more praise, but she, too, read very little of it. It seemed to bore her.

But Mr. Blamires was very enthusiastic. He read every page with great care and praised all that he read. 'It's wonderful, Francis,' he said. 'There are not many lads of your age that can put a magazine like this together. Look at that—a beautiful little drawing. When are we going to see a second number?'

Francis had not yet thought of a second number but immediately his head began to fill with plans—another article on 'I Lived Then', a page of instructions—this time by Alfred the Saxon, more puzzles and jokes.

' And what about a contribution from me this time ? ' asked Mr. Blamires.

' Do you write things about History then, Mr. Blamires ? '

' Not exactly. But have a look at this.'

He went to a cupboard and took out a notebook. It was not like the cheap notebooks that Francis had seen on sale in Durham, it was more like the sketch-book his aunt Elizabeth had shown him. When Mr. Blamires opened it Francis saw that some of the pages were covered with small handwriting.

' Now then, what about a poem for your magazine ? '

' Do you write poems, Mr. Blamires ? '

' I used to, but I don't write many now.'

' Read one out for me, will you ? '

Mr. Blamires put on his spectacles and began to read—

> ' The caller goes from door to door.
>   " Get up, get up ! " he cries.
> The night is dark, the night is cold,
>   But I must wake and rise.
>
> ' The moon and stars pass overhead,
>   The cold wind makes no sound ;
> But the wind does not stir and the stars do not shine
>   Where I work underground.

' There now, what do you think of that ? '

' I think it's wonderful. Did you really make it up by yourself ? '

' Yes, but a long time ago.'

Francis begged Mr. Blamires to read him more poems, and when *Looking Back No.* 2 was finished, on the middle page there was an important heading—

' IMPORTANT ANNOUNCEMENT
These poems were sent to the editor by Mr. M. Blamires,
26 Queen Street, Hesleyside Colliery. '

Under the heading was copied the little poem about the caller and this second poem—

' This is my home, and this the place
Where all my wandering ends.
And this is where I find at last
My work, my wife, my friends.

Dark are the streets. The cold wind blows
Through hawthorn and through oak ;
But I will live and I will die,
With the canny collier folk.'

While they sat looking through the magazine, discussing their
plans for another number, Mrs. Blamires lay puffing and sighing
on her bed, rustling her papers, folding them over and letting
them slide like avalanches down the steep slopes of her bed. But
from time to time she would look up to listen.

' What about coming a bit up to date, Frankie ? Put something
with a bit of gossip into it—about Lord Nelson and Lady
Hamilton.'

' That would be a good idea, Mrs. Blamires.'

' And what about something from Mrs. B. for a change ? I
can give you a good tip for the Oaks or the Derby—a good long-
shot. What about that now ? I bet folks will look at your paper
if they think they'll find a few tips in it.'

Francis did not know what to say to her. He had grown very
fond of her and did not wish to offend her, but he didn't like the
idea of putting racing tips in his magazine.

' Thank you very much, Mrs. Blamires,' he said. ' They would
be very nice, if we had room for them.'

' Yes,' she went on. ' I can give you a good outsider. A sure
runner and a good price. That'll make your father prick up his
ears now, won't it ? '

But the tips never appeared. Nor did any more poems.
Before the third number was completed, a sad and unexpected
disaster drove all thoughts of the magazine from Francis's head.

24

The Accident

FRANCIS was cupboard monitor for his class, and stayed behind when school was over to see that all the books were back in the cupboard and to give the keys to the teacher. When he could not find his teacher he stood outside the room in which the staff collected after school, waiting for him to turn up. He knocked and asked for Mr. Hall, but he was not in the room, and Francis settled down to wait for him.

After a while the door opened and Mr. Cresswell came out.

' You still waiting here, Kirtley ? '

' Yes, sir, I'm waiting to give the keys to Mr. Hall.'

' Why didn't you ask me to take them ? '

' I didn't think it was right, sir.'

' Hand them over to me now. You've waited long enough. I'll see Mr. Hall gets them.'

Francis handed them over to him gratefully, and went out through the big porch. He was the last to leave school and the big clay-covered playground was empty. There was a silence over everything. The silence that had come over the deserted school seemed to spread outwards, over the playground to the squat colliery rows with the stolid grey sky pressing smokily down upon the dark roofs.

He walked across the playground, out through the wooden gate, along the great blunt wall that enclosed the school; then, as he turned the corner of Russell Street, he saw that a number of boys had collected somewhere in the middle of the street, near his aunt Elizabeth's. They were crowding round the colliery ambulance. The doors of the ambulance had been left open, and he could not see whether someone had been brought to the house or was being taken from it. On the opposite side of the street stood a group of women, gathered as they always were when the dreaded ambulance appeared. Their faces were drawn and anxious, and some of them had thrown their aprons back over their shoulders to fend off the cold evening air.

When Francis got home his mother was not there, but his father was sitting at the table. He was still black from the pit, and his meal was laid out before him, but he was not eating. The pit dirt covered his face like a mask, but Francis could see from his eyes that he was troubled.

'What's happened, da?'

'Something terrible, Francis. Dinna gan anywhere near your aunt Elizabeth's. Not for a bit anyway. Not till we hear from your mother.'

'Has somebody been hurt in the pit?'

'Aye.'

'Is it my uncle?'

'No, it's David. They've just fetched him back badly hurt.'

'What happened to him?'

'Oh a terrible thing. He was riding inbye on the set, and something seems to have gone wrong with the switches. Anyhow the set took a turning into one of the low seams . . . The number of lads killed riding on that set . . . it's terrible.'

Francis knew what his father meant. The 'set' was the long train of tubs that was hauled by machinery from the working places to the bottom of the shaft and then back again. Often the men rode on it, but they had to go with care and many an accident had happened with it.

'It looks as if our David was riding on the front tub, and when the set jumped the rails it flung him off. The others are not badly hurt, but . . . they say there's not much chance for him.'

He turned back to his meal but he could not eat anything. Together they filled the bath, and Mr. Kirtley began to wash himself. Neither felt like speaking. They waited in silence until, late in the evening, Mrs. Kirtley came in.

'What's he like then, Dot?' asked her husband.

'He's finished, Simon.'

'What, has he gone?'

'Not yet, but he hasn't come round. He winna come round again. I can see it.'

'Was it the set that did it?'

'Yes . . . just an accident, Simon, that's the pity.'

'Are you going back to sit up with Elizabeth?'

'I'll have to, Simon. Jacob's worse than useless at a time like this, and Elizabeth cannot go through this by herself. Ye'll have to look after yourselves tonight. Can you manage?'

'We'll manage, Dot. Dinna worry about us.'

'You get off to bed, Francis. No, now dinna start asking questions. Just keep out of the way, pet, 'cos this is a bad time for all of us.'

Francis went off to bed. He thought he would not sleep but he did. It was light when he woke. He got up, lifted the skylight of his attic and looked out across the street. The blinds were up in all the houses in the opposite street, except one. He knew that his cousin was dead.

Suddenly the cold of the clammy lino seemed to strike up through his body. He felt as if both his heart and his breathing were about to stop, and looking down he saw that his hands had gone pale and a queer blueness was spreading over the nails. He let the skylight fall and the glass broke and fell on to the attic floor. But he had to get back in bed, where he lay shivering, untouched by the warmth of the bedclothes.

When his mother called him he tried to get up but the power had gone out of his limbs and a strange fatigue such as he had never felt before came over him. As he came downstairs he felt his legs giving way under him, and when he caught sight of himself in the looking-glass he was shocked to see how white and drawn he was. He had never had a headache in his life, but now there was a pain in his brow, his temples and the back of his head as if something hard and spiky had been jammed on his skull. School was out of the question. His mother lit a fire in the 'room', and made up a bed for him on the sofa.

As he lay there looking into the fire and trying to find a comfortable position, he could hear his father and mother talking.

'In a way it's a godsend our Francis is off colour. He would want to have a last look at his cousin, but I dinna want him to see him.'

'Is he as bad as that?'

'Oh Simon, it makes my heart bleed to look at him.'

'And he was one of the nicest looking lads you could see anywhere.'

'Not now, Simon. You wouldn't recognize him . . . so it's just as well that our Francis is in bed.'

Francis trembled as he heard them talking. The image of his dead cousin kept coming back to him. He could not stop re-enacting in his own mind the swift ride through the blackness of the pit, and the sudden blow from nowhere that had driven the life and handsomeness from his cousin. It was only after the doctor had been and made him swallow a few tablets that he was able to sleep.

He was still in bed on the day of the funeral. Both doctor and mother had forbidden him to get up. After they had gone he lay in bed listening to the bickering of the sparrows in the gutters, the cackling of a hen in somebody's garden and the long swooping whistles of the starlings. The 'room' was at the back of the house, and he could neither hear nor see the preparations for the funeral; but at last he heard the mourners begin upon a hymn and he got up, went into the kitchen and stood on the form to see out of the window. The pale coffin had been brought out and was standing on two chairs in the street. The coffin shone like corn in the sunshine, but the suits and dresses of the men and women were as black as coal, as black as the horses yoked to the polished hearse.

> 'Safe in the arms of Jesus,
> Safe on his loving breast—'

sang the mourners, and the sound of their singing was thin and shrill. They had no hymn-books, and there were few who knew the words of all the verses. The hymn ended with a thin whispering of song. Then the coffin was lifted from the chairs and put into the hearse. Then the bandsmen lifted their instruments and began to play the music they always played when one of their members had died—the Dead March. The piercing music entered Francis's body like blades. His flesh pimpled and he began to shiver. All his grief for his cousin came flooding into his eyes and he laid his head on the kitchen table.

When the funeral was over and the routine of the colliery began to reassert itself, Francis recovered a little and was anxious to go back to school. He did not like having to stay in bed. He wanted to be up, wrestling with his weakness rather than giving in to it. But for days he was still shaky and slow, and vexed with himself for being so uncertain. He had always prided himself on being at the top of the class, but now he felt he was lagging behind, that he had missed, while he had been ill, something that he could not make up.

He threw himself into his work, determined to forget his grief in the effort to make up for what he had missed, but from time to time the shock that he had felt when he had seen the blinds drawn and realized that David was dead, would return to him. His mind seemed to come to a stop. He could not concentrate for thinking of the unbearable details of his cousin's accident. He hardly knew where he was and what he was doing.

One day they were doing French, not with Mr. Curry who was away from school, but Mr. Cresswell. Mr. Cresswell did not quite know what to do with them, but he said they could sing a few songs for him. At first Francis enjoyed the singing, but when one of the boys asked if they could sing ' *J'avais un camarade* . . .' he felt the tears come into his eyes and his whole body begin to shake. After the first few lines he sat down, buried his head on the hard, cold desk, and began to cry. As he cried he heard the voices of the class die away.

' What is it, Francis ? ' said Mr. Cresswell. It was the first time he had ever used his christian name.

' What is it ? Has something upset you ? '

'He's thinking about his cousin, sir,' said one of the boys. 'He was killed, sir, in the pit, last week, sir.'

'Is that it?' asked Mr. Cresswell.

Francis moved his head up and down.

'And was it the song that upset you?'

Francis nodded again.

'No more singing then, all of you. Come on, get out your slates and we'll do some sums . . . You, boy, take Francis Kirtley out and let him sit in the porch until he feels better.'

He sat with his back against the radiator, with the caps and coats of his schoolfellows ranged mutely around him, and gradually he stopped crying. He wanted to go back into the classroom, but not until all traces of his tears had gone. He filled one of the cracked handbasins with water, dipped his face into it as he had seen his grandfather do, and began to wipe himself on the rough towel. He had just finished when the porch door opened and the caretaker came in. He was a rough old man who went by the nickname of Billy Fineday, because no matter what the weather was his first words of the day were always 'Fine day, Mr. Cresswell. Fine day, Mr. Curry.'

Francis jumped when he saw him come in. He had a great fear of being found out and thought for a moment that the old man had discovered who it was that had taken the grappling-hooks from his boiler-house. He was relieved when he heard him say, 'What's up, Frankie? Been getting into trouble?'

'No,' said Francis. He did not want to confess that he had been crying. 'I just felt a bit queer and I came out to get a drink. What's that you've got?'

The caretaker had a pigeon in his hand. He was holding it with the tail pointing away from him, and with the bird's legs lightly trapped between his fingers. 'Just a stray,' he said. 'I picked it up last week on the boiler steps. Lad, it was in a bad way.'

'Is it hurt?'

'It was, but I've given it a bit of corn and I've patched it up. There was summat wrang with one of its legs, but I've mended it.'

He turned the bird over and showed Francis where he had put a splint on its left leg.

' Is it all right now ? Can it fly ? '

' It'll fly, right enough. Look at its flipes.'

He spread the wings out one by one and showed Francis how sound they were.

' It's wonderful the way they come round if you look after them and show a bit of kindness. It's as right as the mail now.'

' Are you going to keep it ? '

' Nay, I mustn't do that. It will have a home of its own somewhere or other.'

' Are you going to let it off now ? '

' Aye. Want to watch it ? '

' Yes.'

' Come on afore the teacher catches ye.'

He opened the porch door and went outside. Then he lifted his hand above his head and threw the bird very lightly into the air. It struck out immediately. Francis could see the damaged leg trailing a little but the wings beat strongly and confidently. It circled once round the playground and then flew off.

' There it goes,' said Billy. ' It will manage. It will be safe in its own ducket afore it's dark.'

They stood watching the bird until it was out of sight.

' See ? ' said the old man. ' It dissent tak' them lang to get over their troubles if ye just have a bit of patience with them. Are you feeling better yourself, hinny ? '

' Yes, I'm all right now, Mr. Fineday,' said Francis and they both laughed at the nickname.

When Francis went back into the classroom he saw the eyes of all the class raised to look at him and see if he was still crying, but Mr. Cresswell said, ' Come on now, all of you, just get on with your work.'

Francis went back to his seat and took up his pen. The blackboard was covered with problems, but as soon as he had read through them he knew he could do them. He set to work and wrote fast and confidently.

25

Francis Recovers

DAY by day Francis grew stronger. His best doctors were
Mr. Cresswell, who looked after him and went out of his way
to make him happy at school, and Mr. Blamires, who played
checkers with him and took him out, patiently diverting his mind
from his loss. His aunt Elizabeth gave him David's famous
county cap and he added it to his collection of treasures. He
put it in a drawer with two poems that Mr. Blamires had copied
out for him, and his uncle's album of war photographs.

One day Mr. Cresswell showed the class a little wireless set he
had made. He took it to pieces, demonstrated how easy it was
to build, and told them about the kind of things he could get
from it. From then on Francis desired a wireless set more than
anything else in the world. Remembering how he had managed
to get the missing volumes of the *Book of Knowledge*, he started
to help once more the old woman who kept the fish-shop, and
saved up his earnings to buy first the copper wire for the cylinder,
then the condenser, then the cat's whisker and the crystal. When
he got to this stage, his father helped him to buy the earphones.
He set up his receiver in the sitting-room, much to the displeasure
of his mother, who did not like the aerial wire trailing from
picture to picture, and he spent many cold hours there trying to
pick up messages. There were as yet no regular programmes on
the air, but from time to time he picked up mysterious and
fascinating sounds—the first that he had ever heard from the
world outside Hesleyside. When he called his father in to listen
to something, Mr. Kirtley invariably spoilt it by fiddling with
the cat's whisker, trying to find a better spot on the crystal, but
day by day Francis grew more expert at managing the set; and

on one wonderful evening he sat listening to the sound of a nightingale being broadcast from a wood somewhere in the south of England. No nightingales came as far north as Hesleyside. This was the first he had ever heard.

Then one Saturday not long after he had gone back to school there came to Russell Street an important letter. The sight of the bulky foolscap envelope alarmed him at first. Its official appearance made him think that the law had at last caught up with him and this was the long-delayed summons; but the letter had come, not from the police, but from the Director of Education, and informed him that if he wished to accept it there was a place for him in the Durham Johnston School. His father had to sign the form if he wished to accept the place.

The next day both Mr. Blamires and Grandpa came to tea, and by way of celebration the table was laid in the 'room'. Mr. Kirtley did not like to have tea there, but his wife was proud of her son and, partly to celebrate his success, and partly to please her father, who did not like to treat the Sabbath as if it was no different from any other day of the week, she lit a fire and took out one of her best table-cloths. She removed the wireless aerial, sponged down the leaves of her aspidistra and took out all her treasured photographs of her father when he had first been made Superintendent of the Sunday School, herself and her husband on their wedding day, her dead brothers in their khaki uniforms, and David in his county cap. The room looked cosy and comfortable for once.

They all sat down at the big table, the old man in his spruce Sunday best, Mr. Kirtley in his shirt sleeves. His wife had persuaded him to put on a collar and tie but he would not wear his jacket.

'Let us ask God's blessing on this good news, Simon,' said the old man as they sat down at the table. 'Praise be to the Lord. He has seen fit to take one of my grandsons from me, but in His mercy He has raised up another to great things. Praise be.'

But Mr. Kirtley did not seem inclined to join in the thanks-giving.

'He's done very well,' he said rather grudgingly. 'But this has come at a bad time.'

'What do you mean?' asked the old man.

'We're not as flush as we might be, Grandpa. What with short time and poor wages, we're a bit short. And this'll take money.'

'You're not going to tell me that you'll let that stand between your son and his advancement, are you? Have you no pride in him and what he's done?'

'I'm proud all right, but it's the expense that worries me.'

'What expense?'

'He'll want some new things and a new school-bag, and a good few other things. Man, there's a list there as lang as my arm.'

'Hout, you'll never miss it.'

'If things were what they used to be, I'd never hesitate. But it's nae good shutting our eyes to the facts. There's collieries closing down all over the county. The whole industry's in a bad way. The way things are shaping we'll be the next to get our notices.'

' And what sort of future is there for him if the grown men can't find work ? '

' He's got a good headpiece. There's many a shop that would be glad of a lad with his talent.'

' I'm ashamed of you, Simon, talking like this. Are you going to be as sackless as that other son-in-law of mine ? If he hadn't have been in such a rush to get his son off to work, David would never have been killed the way he was.'

Mr. Kirtley did not answer immediately, but sat pulling uneasily at the ends of his moustaches. He hated being un-generous in any way, but the prospect of being out of work troubled him.

' It's all very well for you to talk, Grandpa,' he said, but there was not very much conviction in his voice. ' I'm the one that has to foot the bill.'

All through the conversation Mr. Blamires had not spoken. He did not break his silence until the old man had gone and Francis and his mother were also out of the room.

' Simon,' he said. ' I didn't say anything when you were talking with Grandpa. It's not my business to interfere in things that don't concern me. But now that we're by ourselves, there's something that I want to say to you.'

' Go ahead, Michael,' said Simon. He was still tugging nervously at the end of his moustache. ' You're my marra. I wouldn't like you to keep anything back.'

' I didn't want to say this, Simon, because it means telling you something I'm not supposed to tell you . . . Do you know who it was that saved you from trouble with the police about that gun ? '

' I have nae idea.'

' It was the very lad you've just been talking about.'

' What, our Francis ? '

' Yes.'

' Nivver ! '

'He didn't do it on his own—that stands to reason—there was twenty or thirty involved in this. But he was the ringleader—him and your poor David. A few days before the policeman went to drag the quarry, the boys got the gun out and made sure it would never be found again.'

'Where did they put it?'

'That's immaterial. The main fact is that if it hadn't been for Francis, you would all have been up before the magistrate—Toast and Matty Howden—the lot of you.'

'Well, of all the daring little beggars! And he's kept it under his hat all these months! How did you get to know?'

'Never mind about that, Simon. That's my little secret. But there it is—and I thought I ought to tell you.'

'Lad, tha mak's me ashamed of myself, Michael. Here I've been worrying and shilly-shallying about a few shillings—and he's saved me pounds. No, I dinna mean that. It's not the money that matters . . . Here, give me that pen, Michael. I'll see that he gets his chance even if I never drink another sup.'

Mr. Blamires waited until the letter had been signed and the envelope sealed. Then he took another envelope from his pocket, and put it on the table. 'That's something else I want you to see, Simon,' he said, 'but it's not to be opened till Dot comes in and I've gone.'

A few minutes later Mrs. Kirtley came in. She had brought her sister Elizabeth with her for a bite of something to eat. Simon told them what he had learnt about Francis and the gun, and then opened the letter. It was hardly a letter. It was written in pencil on a sheet torn from the book which Mrs. Blamires kept for her notes on horses.

'I want you to use what I've put in this letter for Francis. I've just had a bit of luck on the geegees, and one or two handy little bets have come up for me. I wouldn't rest if the lack of a few pounds came in between your little lad and his big chance. If only Michael had had somebody to stand by him at the right time he wouldn't have been where he is now. I want you to use this for his bits of things, because from what I hear he'll want them if he is to get off on the right foot. With the best of luck to a lad that's been good company to a bed-ridden woman with no bairns of her own.

Bella.'

With the message was a five-pound note.

'We canna tak' this, Dot,' said Mr. Kirtley. 'Michael's my marra. He gets the same paynote that I get.'

'Take it, Simon,' said Elizabeth. 'It's not from Michael, it's from Bella.'

'Even then, I'd think a thousand shames of myself if I took charity like this. A man likes to stand on his own feet.'

'Take it,' went on Elizabeth. 'Take it and don't be so proud. If anybody had given our David a chance like this and I'd stood in his way, I would never have forgiven myself.'

Simon looked up at her and saw that her eyes were filling with tears.

'Mebbe you're right, Elizabeth,' he said. 'We wasted the life of one of our lads. God forbid that we should waste the other. Here, tak' the money, Dot. You'll need it.'

When the letter had finally been sent off, Francis went to see Mr. Blamires.

'Well, Francis,' said Michael, 'now you're all fixed up. You may not think so, but I was like you when I was your age. I was sharp. I wanted to be somebody, and I knew that I had it in me, but I never got the chance to prove it. Poverty, and nobody to stand by me just at the right moment—that was my undoing. I had to work hard just to keep alive—just to make sure I had something to eat and somewhere to sleep. Listen to this. This is something I put down long afterwards when I came to think back over those days.

" All day I walk the lonely roads.
I beg like a dog for a bone.
I have no brother, no father, no mother.
I live and sleep alone."

'—that's poetry, but it's true as well. It was a bad time for me. I got over it. But when I came in the end to Hesleyside and had a home of my own and a wife of my own, it was too late.'

'But you're a poet, Mr. Blamires. You write poems and they're as good as any in the poetry books.'

'You're the only one that thinks so, bonny lad. No, I'll live and die a pitman. It's too late for me to do anything different. But you've got everything in front of you. You can grow up to be a distinguished man—not like us poor miners that nobody seems to care about nowadays. We haven't much of a future—but you can be somebody—somebody that your father and mother and Mrs. Blamires and me will be proud of one day.'

Francis was a little embarrassed at his words. He felt that it was a great responsibility to have hopes such as these pinned on him. Yet he knew in his heart that he would never now be what fate had condemned his father and Mr. Blamires to be. What he would become he did not know, but he knew that another destiny was drawing near to him, and that if only he did not betray his true self he would enter upon it.

'That poem you just recited, Mr. Blamires,' he said. 'Did you finish it?'

'No, there's another verse.'

'Say it for me.'

> 'Nothing is mine but the thoughts I think.
> These are my heritage,
> Though I put them down with a borrowed pen
> Upon a borrowed page.

'—but yours won't be a borrowed pen or a borrowed page either. They'll be your own. And some day folk will listen to those thoughts of yours.'

26

Mr. Cresswell says Good-bye

In June the school had a half-day holiday for the regatta that was held every year in Durham. When they had been better off Mr. Kirtley had taken Francis to see the racing, but this year there was no hope of his getting there. However there was one feature of the regatta that the boys could enjoy without spending any money. The races always ended with a fireworks display. Francis had never seen it at close quarters for even in the prosperous years there was no way of getting home from Durham except by walking, and the display ended too late to think of that. But the boys had found out long ago that it was possible to see at least the rockets going up if they went up to a place in the fields between the colliery and the village, and for years it had been the custom for them to gather there and watch them rising over the far skyline.

As soon as the light had gone out of the sky they collected at their favourite spot, Nocky Howden, the two Ords and most of the boys who had helped to hide the gun—squabbling and fighting and shouting, but always with one eye on the horizon, waiting for the first rocket to burst. Francis sat with his back to the stone wall, jumping up from time to time to join in the fun, but always going back to his place to scan the darkening sky. Behind him the brilliant colours of the sunset drained away from the western sky, and the lights of far collieries began to appear like pinpricks. The moths began to rise from the long grasses, and a star or two appeared, shy and wavering. Then at last the first rocket went up, and all the boys began to shout and cheer.

They all huddled against the wall, their eyes fixed on the far sky, and watched the inaudible rockets bursting and opening, showering upwards and outwards in explosions of green and silver and crimson, then falling and fading, extinguishing themselves with lingering slowness. To Francis they were like signals from another country, silent and beautiful gestures from an unknown and welcoming land. One brilliant explosion followed another, the rockets leaping into the air like brilliant fish rising from a dark sea, glittering in the darkness and then falling back into the element from which they had sprung.

But little by little the night grew darker and colder, and the intervals between each brilliant explosion grew longer and longer. One by one the boys broke away and began to return to the colliery. Francis stayed on, hoping to see one more rocket, drawing into his nostrils the smell of the damp fields and the fading hawthorn blossom, looking down upon the flickering lights of the collieries. He was the only one left there. He lingered a little longer, but at last he turned to go. He ran down the hill feeling the wetness of the fields strike through his thin boots, and the softness of the yielding turf give way to the cinders and ashes of the colliery streets.

When he came into the house he saw his father sitting on a cracket trying to put a new sole on a pair of boots that had worn through. He had taken to doing his own cobbling to save a few pennies, although he was not very expert, and the soles he was putting on were not of leather but of rubber cut from an old motor tyre. Many of the men were having to do jobs like these for themselves.

' Did you see the fireworks, then, bonny lad ? ' he asked.

' Yes, da.'

' And did you enjoy them ? '

' Yes, they were lovely.'

' I bet they were. It's a bit since we had a day out at the regatta, isn't it ? Ah well, things have to get worse afore they get better. They might pick up a bit in the next few months. We never died in winter yet.'

But he looked a little despondent, and before Francis went to bed his mother told him that the caller had been round again, and the pits had been laid idle until further notice.

All through June and July trade was bad and there was talk of closing the pit, but it stayed open, with the men working short time and everyone living on short commons. Fortunately news came that the Education Committee was giving a grant to boys who were going to the Grammar School. It was not much but it made Francis feel that at least he was contributing something to the family funds. He had been happy at Hesleyside School and was sorry to be leaving it, but he looked forward to the holiday and the prospect of the Grammar School.

The Headmaster of Hesleyside never made a fuss about the last day of term. He liked to keep the classes working until the last minute; but at the end of the last day, when they gathered for prayers, instead of singing ' Now the day is over ' as they habitually did on the last day of the week, he chose 'Lord, dismiss us with Thy blessing '. This was always the signal that the term had really come to an end. It was the order of release and the children sang it with great gusto. Even the teachers seemed to be infected by the excitement of breaking up, and smiled at one another as the sound of the singing swelled. When the hymn ended there was a brief moment of reluctant silence for the benediction, and then the children rushed out of the school like prisoners whose term was up.

Francis stayed behind to see that the cupboards were locked and to hand in the keys for the last time. Most of the teachers were still in the big room where they had had prayers but Mr. Cresswell was in the porch that served as the staff-room. He was packing his things away in a big case. Francis saw him take out his football boots and put them in a brown paper bag. They were the boots he wore when he was training the team.

' Well, Francis,' he said. ' This is your last day, isn't it ? '

' Yes, sir.'

' The last time you'll hand in the keys.'

' Yes, sir.'

' You haven't spoken to me about your uncle recently. Does he still live with you ? '

'No, sir, he's not working in Hesleyside now. He's working in Yorkshire, sir, at Saltburn.'

'Then I don't suppose I shall see him again. I don't suppose I shall see you either.'

'I'll come back to see you, Mr. Cresswell.'

'I'm afraid you won't find me here.'

'Are you leaving as well, sir?'

'Yes, I'm leaving Durham. No more coal mines for me. I'm going south.'

'Are you going to be a Headmaster, sir?'

'Yes, I am.'

'I bet you'll have a good football team there, sir.'

'No, I don't think so. My footballing days are over.'

He fell silent for a moment, then folded the bag containing his boots and put it in his case.

'I've never said this to anyone, Francis, but when your cousin was killed, it was a great loss to me. He was a great player and I thought that one day I would be able to say to myself . . . yes, I discovered him and I trained him. Would you like a little souvenir before you leave us?'

'Yes, sir.'

'It isn't much, but you may like it. It's the letter I got telling me that David was to play for the county.'

He took the letter out of his wallet and handed it to Francis, and as he did so he turned and looked up at the cup that was still standing on the shelf where it had been put after the game.

'It's a nice cup,' he said. 'Sooner or later it will have to go. But keep the letter. For auld lang syne, shall we say?'

When Francis was putting the letter among his other treasures he could not help thinking of the day when Mr. Cresswell had taken them for Scripture and had been vexed with him for not knowing what the 'head of the corner' was. He did not think that he would ever be sorry to see him go. Now he knew that without David and the man who had trained him and the other players, Hesleyside school would never be the same. He was ready now for a new beginning.

The Big Meeting

IT was the last Saturday in July, the day of the ' Big Meeting ', as it was called, when men and women and children from every colliery in the county crowded together in the narrow streets of Durham. So many came that the city had to be closed to traffic for the day. Early in the morning the police cleared the streets, and put up barriers at the city entrances, and from then on until late in the evening no vehicles were allowed in the streets. All through the morning and the early part of the afternoon the delegations from the collieries with their bands and bandsmen assembled at the upper end of North Road, hoisted their banners and paraded through the city, crossing the bridge, climbing the narrow slope of Silver Street and passing through the market-place until they came to the field by the river where the platforms had been erected for the speakers. This was the great Miners' Gala, and for one day the ancient city was theirs.

Francis and his father had walked into Durham to see the procession of bands and banners. They had come by the way that Francis had taken when he had come for his interview, and they took their stand at the bottom of North Road, a position from which they could see both the street and the road across the bridge. Behind them sloped the cobbled street that led to the Johnston School, and on the far side of the bridge rose the walls of the castle and the Cathedral towers.

The pavement was crowded and from time to time Francis was pushed into the gutter by the crowds behind him, but he jostled his way back so that he could stand on the curb and see over the heads of the folk in front of him. As the procession came past, the people around him shouted greetings above the noise of the bands to their friends. Francis saw the men who were carrying the banners take their hands for a second or two from the poles and wave back to the crowds. The wind was catching the banners, filling them like sails, and making the poles sway. From time to time the crowds on the far side parted a little, and Francis saw the boards that the shopkeepers had nailed across the shop fronts to protect the glass from the pressure of the thousands who filled the street.

As the banners went by he read the names of the collieries— Pelaw, Washington, Medomsley, Sleetburn, Oakenshaw, Sacriston, Cornsay, Bloemfontein, Craghead, Dean and Chapter, Langley Park . . . The banners were brilliantly coloured in blues and reds and golds, all tasselled and decorated with portraits of miners' leaders and legendary figures. From time to time one came past draped in black with a heavy black band looped from the cross-bar. It was a sign that in the year since the last Big Meeting someone had been killed in the pit.

At last the Hesleyside banner appeared. The bandsmen were all in the uniform that David had worn, and they were playing a tune that Francis had often heard them practising in the little broken-down room on the edge of the colliery. Some of the banners were new, but Hesleyside still had the one that had been made for them during the war. On the side that was showing there was a picture of Brancepeth Castle. The castle had been used as a convalescent hospital during the war, and the device showed the green lawns in front of the castle gate dotted with the figures of wounded and convalescent soldiers, all in their strange blue uniforms. Above the picture ran, in bold gold letters, the slogan—

UNITY IS STRENGTH

but the lettering was partly hidden by the big crepe ribbon that hung in heavy swags from the cross-pole.

Francis did not need to ask what it was for. The one who had died in the pit was his cousin who ought to have been there among his fellow bandsmen but was now lying in the windy cemetery on the edge of the fells.

Afterword

This second book by my husband on Durham is again based on Brandon, being given the name of Hesleyside. After the war we moved to Worcester, and once away from Durham, he had an overpowering urge to write about his birthplace. Even in those days, he felt that someone should make a record of the old collieries before they vanished without trace. The characters, as in most fiction, are partly imaginary and partly fact. The account of Francis answering all the questions in the preliminary examination for the 'scholarship' as it was then called, and the interview at the Grammar School close by the cathedral actually happened to my husband. The grandfather resembled my grandfather — a deeply religious, private sort of person — very erect — and able to walk for miles with no effort, even up to the age of 93. I remember people coming to his house for pills when they were ill — for which he never charged. What went into them, I can't imagine, but I can still see them being rolled in a kind of white powder — was it icing sugar? I was too young to show much interest. Thomas was taken from my husband's uncle whose wife had actually disappeared while he was in France during the 1914–18 war. Mr Blamires is partly based on a very dear friend of my family's. Every night he came to our house where entertainment was of the home produced kind — playing the piano, singing hymns and songs, and then came the turn of Mr Blamires. He enthralled us for hours with his Scottish ballads and Robbie Burns, never needing a book for reference. His prodigious memory never failed to impress me. How had such a person come to live in a mining village? One day he told me that he had been the son of a priest and an actress. They had left him as a baby in Glasgow, promising to send money for his keep. They were never seen again, and were supposed to have emigrated to America. After eight years the money ceased and he was turned out to fend for himself. The collieries in Durham were at their height, attracting men from all over the country, and by some means he found himself there too. In spite of such hardships, he stood apart as a natural scholar and gentleman, a born actor, with a beautiful voice. To him, I owe my love of the spoken word. Nocky was a real person — the author's uncle —

an eccentric who refused to conform — in spite of countless beatings, he resisted all attempts to force him to attend any school or to do any work. After one of these efforsts he did actually hide in a drift. He managed to live to a great age, asking nothing more than to be allowed to walk on the fells alone with nature. It didn't stop him from saying about the young people when he was in his seventies, 'Ah the young people won't have work nowadays.' My husband kept a journal from 1936 onwards, snippets of which went into his books. He loved the art of writing, and had a great will to achieve some sort of personal distinction. Allow the author to speak for himself now, in passages which I have copies from his journals.

24th December 1966
I have worked well, and have today ended my revision of 'The Oak and the Ash'. I am reasonably satisfied with this now. A good deal of pruning has been done — a ruthless cutting away of adjectives etc. I dearly wish to be a widely accepted writer of Children's Books.

Christmas morning 1966, 1 am (after returning from the midnight service)
I don't feel tired. Perhaps what I am most delighted about is that I think I have revised my second Durham story to satisfaction. What will become of it? OUP will publish it, I'm sure. Yes, it's a reasonable achievement now. Perhaps I could revise the sun scene — but shall I touch it again? I'm not sure. I am very anxious that it should be a worthy book.

31st January 1966
Tonight I feel excited about this work. And this is my happiness — to feel something growing and taking shape in me. I am a creator. Creation is my happiness! A maker!

23rd February 1967
A letter from Miss Mabel George is pasted into the notebook, accepting 'The Oak and the Ash' for publication.

Underneath is written:—
    'A most important letter for me!'

Archway Novels

The Poacher's Son by Rachel Anderson	0 19 271545 3
Friend Fire and the Dark Wings by J G Fyson	0 19 271539 9
Terry on the Fence by Bernard Ashley	0 19 271537 2
The Oak and the Ash by Frederick Grice	0 19 271538 0
Break in the Sun by Bernard Ashley	0 19 271476 7
Revolt at Ratcliffe's Rags by Gillian Cross	0 19 271477 5
Fox Farm by Eileen Dunlop	0 19 271478 3
Collision Course by Nigel Hinton	0 19 271479 1
A Pattern of Roses by K M Peyton	0 19 271499 6
The Bonny Pit Laddie by Frederick Grice	0 19 271498 8
A Midsummer Night's Death by K M Peyton	0 19 271480 5
Moses Beech by Ian Strachan	0 19 271481 3
Frontier Wolf by Rosemary Sutcliff	0 19 271482 1
The Islanders by John Rowe Townsend	0 19 271483 X
The Dark Behind the Curtain by Gillian Cross	0 19 271500 3
The Black Lamp by Peter Carter	0 19 271497 X
The Demon Headmaster by Gillian Cross	0 19 271553 4
Brother in the Land by Robert Swindells	0 19 271552 6